D1492882

WANDERING WOMEN

☆ JOHN COURNOS ☆

19 30

Charles Boni PAPER BOOKS *New York*

WANDERING WOMEN
COPYRIGHT, 1930. CHARLES BONI, JR.

PUBLISHED SEPTEMBER, 1930
MANUFACTURED IN THE UNITED STATES OF AMERICA

C O N T E N T S

WANDERING WOMEN

I

"Mother, I wonder what he's like now!"
The younger woman, of an age between twenty-seven and thirty, with large questioning brown eyes turned to the older one sitting at her side in the Café Dome, and her deep mellow voice expressed something more than mere curiosity. It sounded anxious and troubled.

"I don't know, child. It's hard to tell," came the hesitant response, spoken in a shrill nasal twang identifying the speaker as an American; more precisely a New Englander, to those better acquainted with the shades of the native intonation. "Men change monstrously!" There was a touch of bitterness in the tone in which the phrase was uttered. It was clear that the speaker, a plumpish, good-looking woman of about fifty, who in certain aspects seemed younger than her years, did not intend it to be taken as an abstraction. It was spoken from the heart and hinted at deep intimate experience of an unpleasant nature.

The young woman looked hopelessly at her mother, as if cognizant of the fact that no help could be expected from this quarter. Of medium height, she was attractive and well-formed, and bobbed natural-curled hair framed an unblemished pale face, accentuating its pallor and the almost habitual wistfulness of her eyes.

Mindful of the effect her words produced on her daughter, the elder woman spoke more softly. "I hope Jan hasn't changed. I hope so for your sake. But you know what men are. Brutes. Selfish. Every one of them! All they want is to see how much they can get out of a girl. Then—whew, how I detest them!"

These words broke the spell of depression. The younger woman laughed. There was something infinitely simple and child-like in her laugh. "Poor mummy!" she cried. "They haven't paid much attention to you of late, have they?"

This provoked a protest. "What are you saying, Ethel? ... To be sure, I'm no longer young. Even so, only last week Bibberbaum—who is somebody, you must admit—spent a whole afternoon with me. It was all I could do to make him go!"

"Be careful, mother,"—there was a warning sound in Ethel's voice— "Bibberbaum, it's true, is a great German writer. But he happens to be writing a book with an American woman as one of the leading characters, and he may have reasons of his own for cultivating the company of American ladies!"

"Do you mean to insinuate he's using me for copy? I refuse to believe it!"

"Believe it or not. All the same, I should be careful about anything I said to Bibberbaum," replied Ethel evasively. "He's no keeper of secrets. If you want the Quarter to know anything, all you've got to do is to tell it to Bibberbaum. It saves the trouble of putting it in a newspaper."

"Why? Has he said anything about me?" The mother's voice expressed horror and alarm.

"I shouldn't wonder. What I'm concerned about are the things he's said about me!"

"You? Why, who . . ."

"Never mind who told me. But the person who told me said he had it straight from Bibberbaum. The whole Quarter, I dare say, knows by now all about my love affairs, past and present."

"I told him nothing that wasn't flattering. . . ."

"I'm sure of that. . . . You made a regular Cleopatra out of me!"

"But I made him take a vow of secrecy!"

"I've no doubt. But you know Bibberbaum's technique. He passes on the secret, and the vow too. This is his formula: 'I saw Mrs. Mary Prescott this afternoon, and what d'you think the good lady told me about Ethel? Only I've promised not to tell, so please don't repeat it to any one else!' "

"You're hard on him, Ethel."

"Not at all. . . . I suppose you told him about Jan too!"

Mrs. Prescott averted a guilty gaze. "Nothing to your discredit, dear," she said, after an uncomfortable silence. "In fact—"

"In fact, you gave me the most eloquent testimonials," Ethel finished the sentence for her, and laughed caustically, "and expatiated on how badly such a wonderful creature as I have been treated. Isn't that so?"

"Don't be hard on me, Ethel," pleaded her mother. "After all, I've given up my life to you. I've striven to give you everything I've wanted and not had myself. I've done everything for the best!" Her voice trailed off pathetically.

"I know . . . I know . . ." murmured Ethel, half to herself, and there was just enough pity in the brief words to stab her mother to the heart.

A silence fell between mother and daughter while, with curious eyes, they surveyed the frequenters of the café. They reposed on red plush seats against the wall and sipped Armagnac and black coffee close to the large open windows looking out on the pavement crowded with sitters drinking all manner of liquid concoctions.

The usual Dome clientele met their gaze: Lulu, the
negro model, her head tight-swathed in a red and white
bandanna kerchief, who boasted that without her the
Primitivist movement in painting would have been a
dead failure; Jim Barney, ex-pugilist, the bosom friend
of Anglo-Saxon litterati; Robert Dale, American novelist who a few nights before, goaded on by a wag, created
a sensation, almost culminating in a riot, by jumping on
a table and haranguing the crowd on the wag's arrogance
in comparing him with Flaubert—Who was Flaubert,
anyway? He, Robert Dale, would show those French
dogs how to write! Other scarcely less consequential
figures crowded the cosmopolitan picture, with a generous sprinkling of hangers-on and cocottes. The large
majority were Americans. Indeed, the café had a reputation for attracting an American clientele, a profitable
one, inasmuch as, unlike the Latins, its members did
not linger over drinks, but, like proper he-men, took
them at a single gulp.

Mother and daughter suddenly espied a tall cadaver-
ous figure pausing leisurely in the doorway to survey the
drinkers, as if he were looking for some one. His immense head was partly bald, his formidable Adam's
apple truculently protruded from a long neck, and he
had a prominent beaked nose; altogether, the portrait
was as nearly as possible that of a vulture in human
shape. Oddly enough, when he turned full face his fea-

tures, in the blaze of light, were both amiable and kindly; and there were indications of his having been handsome in his youth. The bluest imaginable eyes, darting innocent glances, looked out from under bristling bushy eyebrows. He might have been anywhere between fifty-five and sixty.

"There's Rennell, mother!" exclaimed Ethel.

It was indeed Wilfred Rennell, the well-known English novelist, of whom in his youth it was said that he'd surpass all his contemporaries. In his own opinion, he had vindicated this prophecy. He could be quite eloquent on the subject. He was sure that posterity would do him the justice denied him in his own day. In his own words, "If you write for posterity, only posterity will read you." And he had come to Paris "to die." Not that he was contemplating death as an imminent visitor. He enjoyed a juicy fillet steak, his wine, after-dinner coffee and cognac far too well to think of dying. He liked French fare, admired all things French, and enjoyed the company of Americans with whom he had several points of contact. To begin with, they showed a "premature" appreciation of his books; premature—his word—in the sense that they appreciated them without waiting, like his own correct countrymen, until he was dead. Then, like himself, they adored Paris, and had come there "to die." It was really extraordinary how many young persons in perfectly good health had come to Paris to die. While waiting for the hypothetical moment, they sensibly prepared for it by thoroughly enjoying the excellent fare provided by French chefs and the attendant inner ablutions contributed by a thousand vineyards and distilleries; making of their *danse macabre* a rather lingering affair but, on the whole, a pleasant one. These young men and women felt flattered that the great man should bestow so much of his time on them. He had known almost everybody worth knowing in his time, and many a celebrity had he called by first name. And he had an inexhaustible store of anecdotes, some of which bore the stamp of having been secured at first hand. But his memory was in some respects poor, and several evenings in his company produced a fair crop of twice-told tales. As his improvisation was good, the versions never quite resembled one another, and a contemptuous wag referred to them as "variations on a single theme."

"I do hope he sees us and joins us!" said Mrs. Prescott, who simply doted on celebrities. Doting on celebrities appeared to be her chief function in life. She performed the function with credit, for the celebrity was never left in doubt of her doting on him. She did this with such an appearance of candor, not to say of ecstasy, effectively tempered by commonsense and practicality of the New England variety, that the object of her adoration, unless he was a grumpy soured individual who already had had a surfeit of the honeyed concoction, immediately succumbed to the blandishments of so palpable an admirer. Old Rennell, in spite of his age and experience, was far from being soured or grumpy; the really nice thing about him was that he was always good-natured. And at no time was he contemptuous of any tribute to his genius, whatsoever its source. And a newcomer, particularly a woman, showing an interest in his book always provided him with a welcome diversion. Ethel had met the great man, but her mother hadn't, and she had been dying to meet him for ages because he was one of two or three celebrities in the colony with an established reputation. And here at last was the long-awaited opportunity.

"My dear, ask him to sit with us," Mrs. Prescott urged her daughter.

"But, mother, I don't particularly want him to sit with us!"

By this time, Rennell had espied Ethel and was making his way between the tables towards them.

Ethel smiled a greeting and gave him a hand which he grasped in his and held while he looked questioningly at her companion.

"This is my mother," said Ethel, withdrawing her hand. His perspiring large hand affected her unpleasantly.

"Pleased to meet you," he said, offering his hand to

Mrs. Prescott, who shook it with an alacrity which made up for her daughter's indifference. "May I sit down?"

"Of course! I shall consider myself honored," said Mrs. Prescott quickly, "if the author of 'Autumn Rains' gives us his company."

"Thank you," he said, sitting down opposite them. "I have a bone to pick with you, Miss Prescott," he said, turning to Ethel.

"Not really?" Ethel glanced at him whimsically.

"But I have!" he pursued. "You've repeatedly ignored my invitation to Monday tea."

"I'm sorry. I had a drawing to finish last Monday."

"Too bad, young lady. You missed something. Legrange, the famous Pointillist, came. And Jennifer, the Sur-realiste. They got into an argument. Well, you know the French. You'd have thought their life depended on it!"

"What do you think of the Pointillists, Mr. Rennell?" asked Mrs. Prescott, thinking she ought to say something.

"Oh, they have their points!" replied Rennell, smiling at his own joke, and looking very shrewd.

"You're punning, Mr. Rennell!" said Ethel, amused. "I thought punning was considered a heinous crime by members of your school."

"Not at all," he defended himself. "That is, not when the pun has a point. And you must admit mine has!"

"Mr. Rennell is quite right," her mother put in. "Only he won't find it so easy to explain the Sur-realistes!"

"What makes you say that, Mrs. Prescott? It's quite easy. The Sur-realistes are s-so r-realistic!" And he laughed immoderately at his triumph.

"You're positively brilliant to-night," Ethel joined in his laughter. "The funny part of it is that your re-marks exactly describe them."

"Of course, they do!" Rennell agreed. He was quite pleased with himself. "So you've read my last book?" he said, turning to Mrs. Prescott.

"Rather!" she exclaimed fervently.

"You sound as if you liked it!"

"Liked it? I simply adored it!"

"If you have a first edition," he said, "I'd advise you to hold on to it! It was quoted a week ago at two guineas, and all because of a petty misprint. I wrote the word dell, and the confounded printer set it up h-e-l-l!"

"How rude of him!" laughed Ethel.

"Yes, wasn't it? . . . What did you like about my book?" he suddenly addressed himself to Mrs. Prescott. "It's the poorest one I've written, you know," he went on, self-deprecatingly.

"You're fishing!" said Mrs. Prescott, coyly.

"I'm really interested, I assure you. I didn't say the book wasn't good. I said it was poor for *me*. . . . Well, what did you like it about it, Mrs. Prescott?"

"Everything! But I liked best the scene in which Hetty runs out in the storm to meet her lover. Poor thing, to have found his wife waiting there for her!"

"Oh, that! That was jolly good, I admit. . . ." Rennell had by this time caught the eye of the waiter and ordered a black coffee and a Calvados.

"I consider it one of the most exquisite passages in the literature of all time!" exclaimed Mrs. Prescott ardently. "I can't write myself," she added modestly, "but I know I'm a very good critic."

"I'm glad you think so!" He referred to the first part of her speech.

"And then the scene in which that wicked Andrew seduces Hetty! I've never read a more subtle seduction in my life. . . ."

"Seductions have to be subtle, Mrs. Prescott," said Rennell, suavely. "Of course, I mean the successful ones. . . ."

"Otherwise, I suppose, they'd be rapes!" put in Ethel truculently.

"Ethel!" cried her mother reproachfully. "You mustn't say such things!"

"She's quite right, quite right," Rennell came to Ethel's aid.

"Frankly, I don't see the difference," Ethel went on in a contrary mood. "I don't like this splitting of hairs. It all comes to the same thing in the end."

It was to be seen that something irritated her. She thought her mother was making a fool of herself. And she had other reasons besides. A sudden revulsion seized her. Oh, how she hated this place, with its hectic atmosphere, its hollow pretense, its smart empty talk! And, oh, how she hated herself for being a part of it, for having no life outside of it! The fatuous fool, she thought. Why did he come here to-night of all nights? Why had he to sit at their table? And her mother! She meant well, and she had done the best for her. But why must she go on like this, slobbering all over a man because he happened to be a celebrity? He wrote well enough, there was no doubt. But as a man, he was simply not worth thinking about. They were all like that, she thought, these artists with their happy-go-lucky ways, satisfied with themselves, charming enough, too, in their fashion, but letting real life go by them. There was something wrong with it all, Ethel could not help thinking. There was of course the life outside. Was that any better? No, no, it wasn't, she had to admit it. Perhaps, it wasn't even as good. What was to be done? That was the worst of it. She wasn't either one thing or another. She wasn't either of the art world or of the business world. She was neither a good American nor a good European.

It had been different when she first became acquainted with this life. She was then young and fresh and innocent, and she had entered upon the new life with enthusiasm, enjoying to the full its freedom and its novelty. Why had all the fun gone out of it? Her life seemed to her as humdrum as that of any bourgeois. It was dull, dull, dull. . . . How could she stand it any longer? She was bored to tears. This talk-talk-talk was at the very instant grating on her nerves. This din-din-din of the vocal cacophony all around her, now rising to a crescendo, now falling to a low-pitched hum-hum-hum passing almost into silence in which individual strident voices could be heard audibly, jarred on her, moved her to distraction. Her nerves were on edge. She needed a rest from all this, she thought. No, she needed no rest. Distressing thoughts had a way of following one if one tried to rest. What she wanted was a new experience, something thrilling, to shock her out of her *status quo* of intolerable dullness. She knew what drove people to take drugs. But she mustn't do it. Simply mustn't. She had such pity for people who took drugs.

"I'm going!" she said, suddenly rising from her seat.

"But, my dear," remonstrated her mother. "Mr. Rennell is *so* interesting! It's being rude to him to go now."

"I am sorry," said Ethel, rather pathetically. "I don't mean to be rude. You'll forgive me, won't you, Mr. Rennell? I've an appointment at the Deux Magots," she lied. Why had one to stay around with people when one didn't choose to? Why had one to lie to them to please them?

"I'm worried about Ethel," said Mrs. Prescott confidentially, secretly relieved to see her daughter go. "She's a strange child!"

"Perhaps she needs a love affair," said Rennell.

"Heavens knows, she can have one. I'm not one for standing in children's ways. And I've never stood in hers."

"A charming girl," said Rennell, with genuine appreciation. Then, after a pause: "I've had the idea that art absorbed her."

"By no means. She hasn't done a stroke of work in months. Says there are too many artists, and that she's bored with it!"

"Quite! I should say she was a sensible girl!" he said perversely.

"How can you say so, Mr. Rennell? I believe in Art! It's a sort of religion with me. I always say it has its priests and high-priests. And its novices too. There can't be too many artists, now can there?"

"No, we can't have too many artists," he agreed equivocally. "You don't think your daughter would like to try some secretarial work, do you?" he asked suddenly.

"I don't know . . ." she said, hesitating.

"Because if she would," he pursued his line of thought, "I have a book to finish by a certain date and need some help. No short-hand required!"

"It's very kind of you, Mr. Rennell," she said. "I will speak to Ethel, though you mustn't count on my influencing her. She usually has her own way."

"Well, bear it in mind," he said, with a casual air.

"I shall!" she replied, without any real intention of doing so. She was aware of his penchant for engaging handsome young women to do his secretarial work; and gossip was always rife on this subject. And Mrs. Prescott very firmly believed that there was never any smoke without fire. Mr. Rennell might be a high-priest of literature. But Ethel, after all, was her own daughter. Not that Ethel was a saint. Far from it. . . . A sudden qualm seized Mrs. Prescott. This "new life" she had chosen for herself and her daughter had not panned out as well as she had hoped. Her daughter was unhappy. This had become a source of endless concern to her. She had to admit to herself that while her mind was free, her emotions were still badly involved in a puritanic "hangover."

"I'm troubled to see Ethel unhappy," she confessed aloud, with unexpected pathos. "I've given her everything. Yes, everything I've wanted myself. . . . You know life and human nature so well. Tell me, d'you think it was wrong of me?" she asked anxiously.

Thus appealed to, Mr. Rennell—in spite of everything, a kind man—replied: "You mustn't fret about such things, Mrs. Prescott. It's been my experience that human beings go their own ways. Environment may alter their experience but not their essential nature. The good remain good, the charming stay charming, the good-natured can't be other than good-natured, and the rogues go their roguish ways. Your daughter is probably passing through a phase, and it will pass. . . ."

"Indeed, I hope so. But suppose it isn't a mere phase, but a permanent state! . . ." She nervously rubbed her hands. "I simply couldn't bear it! I couldn't bear it!"

"Come, come, Mrs. Prescott," he said kindly yet impatiently. "You mustn't give way to feelings,"—he was becoming alarmed at her show of perturbation—"things are never so bad as they seem. The trouble is, you have too much imagination!"

She considered that a compliment, coming as it did from Mr. Rennell. And he was so kind too. Such things worked on her mood, which was reaching a point where confession becomes imperative as a preliminary to the absolution of one's sins. And Mr. Rennell looked very sympathetic, very nice to confess to. He had been father confessor to many undoubtedly in his day. How else, she thought, could he have learned so much about life and human nature—for they filled his books. That sort of thing, she felt, predisposed a man to listen and advise; to become a receptacle of old wives' tales.

Indeed, such was the case. The novelist in Rennell suddenly scented copy. He saw too that this inhibited puritan woman needed but little encouragement, which he was only too ready to give.

"Let's go," he abruptly suggested, "to some quiet little place where we may chat without being disturbed. This place gives me the jibbies! And I know just the spot. I'm the only Anglo-Saxon that's ever penetrated there, I believe," he added, not without pride. "Only you mustn't give it away. I always go there when I get sick of your compatriots and mine, and want to be alone."

She nodded understandingly, and readily agreed to his suggestion. She too knew many people in the Quarter and feared interruption. They were none too soon, for just as they were going through the doorway they were greeted by some common acquaintances. They did not stop to talk to them but slowly filed past the long serried rows of occupied tables.

"All this, somehow, seems strange and unreal to me to-night," said Mrs. Prescott, scanning the hundreds of faces, oddly like those of animated marionettes in a Futurist painting. Bepainted lips, eyes exaggerated to abnormal size by a deft manipulation of tints; here a fantastic headdress intensifying the peculiar features of its wearer to resemble those of a harem favorite; there a woman cadaverously pale—artificially of course —attired all in black, having an appearance startlingly like a nun's, but in her eyes, accentuated by her pallor, there flared a flame which in profane tones spoke its own meaning, to her laughing long-haired male companion in black velvet coat and broad-brimmed black hat. Such were the high points of interest which in disjointed pattern attracted Mrs. Prescott's eyes, while the din of talk in uprising and subsiding waves intermittently rose and fell.

"Yes, it's a pretty rum lot!" she heard Mr. Rennell say, in response; and his words sounded as unreal as the rest.

Another picture rose before her lingering in her vision. It was of a little old white wooden house in the Connecticut hills which bore over its portals the proud figure of 1763—the year it was built. The picture quickly receded, like a meager ghost ashamed of its own absurd attenuation.

But this—*this* was life—life! Hadn't she said it to herself a thousand times? For an instant the lights, the laughter, the tapestry of faces seen in disjointed fragments, the lighted points of cigarettes and the ascending smoke, an isolated gesture here, a woman's crossed leg there, elsewhere a distorted grimace a fit accompaniment to a neighboring discordant laugh, and among it all the gargoyle-like figure of a peanut-vender flaunting a paper-bag and the more swiftly-moving figure of the *garçon* bearing a tray of bottles—all this blended for Mrs. Prescott into one animated picture, a Futurist masterpiece full of paltry details making mock of man.

And, again, there uprose before her the little white house in the Connecticut hills; it crept into the picture, and dissipated it, but not for long. There was a hectic lure about this life which drew her. Like a hill of maggots, it was all very swarming and alive; every maggot there was excruciatingly alive. What lure could the little white house have for her? For anybody? It was to be buried alive. Yes, buried alive. No, she couldn't think of it. She was glad to be here, glad to be on terms of intimacy with the men who were trying to do things in this world, trying to keep the thinning thread of beauty alive.

At this moment was she not walking at the side of Wilfred Rennell whose books were as much talked about in England as in America? Would not this alone make her an object of envy of her acquaintances and friends in Biddlebury, Connecticut, could they but know it? There was of course her daughter. . . . There was a fly in the ointment of her joy. . . . Never was there ointment without the proverbial fly. . . . Yes, yes, she must tell her troubles to Rennell. He knew human hearts. He would understand. He would tell her what to do. Above all, if she had done right or wrong.

Within fifteen minutes the taxi landed them before a café in a little street off the Quai d'Anjou. Outwardly presenting a face undistinguishable from the hundreds of similar places which dot Paris, once you had passed through the front room with its coffee and liqueur bar and tiny tables you were ushered into a largish room in which, seated before tables, against long plush-covered seats, and engaged in animated conversation, were several groups of good-natured gesticulating Latins. They found an unoccupied corner table next to a congenial group of four men of the intellectual type. It was evident they were discussing a serious theme, though one of them, a big jolly fellow with a long flowing beard, punctuated his remarks with fierce guffaws which made one think of Gargantua. There was something refreshing in the sight of these handsome serious-looking men engaged in warm debate; something devilishly healthy in the robust laugh proceeding from the big fellow with the Gargantuan countenance.

"Aren't they a jolly crowd?" Mrs. Prescott was moved to remark.

"Yes, aren't they?" Rennell agreed. "Typical French highbrows. This is one of their meeting-places. They're discussing Proust. The proprietor too is an interesting fellow. See him there with the apron? You wouldn't know to look at him that he served in the Chamber of Deputies. But he has. He's a radical. He runs some vineyards, and some of the best cheaper wines here come from his own place."

"He looks like a shrewd fellow," observed Mrs. Prescott, examining the keen Voltairian features of the middle-aged man in the apron who was approaching to take their order.

Monsieur Lerousse exchanged a greeting with Rennell. "What will you have?" Rennell asked, turning to his companion. "The Calvados is excellent here. And for that matter, the Armagnac!"

"Armagnac for me," she replied. Rennell ordered Calvados.

"What an interesting place!" exclaimed Mrs. Prescott, surveying the other patrons. "What interesting-looking people!"

"Yes. And French as you make 'em. No running down their country, no silly preoccupation with sex, no puritanic inhibitions, no drunkenness. Yet look how their eyes sparkle!"

"No drunkenness?"

"No. I've lived in France a good many years. I've mingled a lot with the natives. And I've yet to meet a drunken Frenchman!"

"How extraordinary!"

"Not at all. The French sip their drinks, they don't gulp them like your countrymen. They drink not to lose themselves in oblivion, but to enliven their spirits and conversation. Look how happy they are, talking on a serious theme! Look at their eyes! Have you seen anything like this at the Dome?"

"It's rather forced there, I should say."

"Exactly. . . . But here comes the girl with the drinks. Have a good look at her!"

She was something to see. A dark, handsome, graceful girl, with resolute face and deep-set intelligent eyes. She might have come to life from an ancient Greek vase. She skillfully poured out a glass of Armagnac to the brim, without spilling a drop. Then she pulled the cork of the other bottle and said in French that her father, Monsieur Lerousse, had just received a new consignment of Calvados. Wouldn't Monsieur like to taste it, or would he prefer the old brand? And she poured out a quarter of a liqueur glass. Rennell, who from his long residence in France passed for a connoisseur in such things, put the glass to his lips and tasted the liqueur drop by drop, lingering over each. The girl watched him with a grave air, scarcely missing the flicker of an eyelash; while Mrs. Prescott intently watched them both. At his gesture of approval, the girl filled his glass, then walked away.

"Did you observe the performance?" he asked.

"Yes."

"To the tiniest detail?"

"Yes. Why?"

"What you saw," he explained, "if you did see it, was the critical spirit of Europe in play. Better still, the nuance of France!"

"Eh? . . ." she murmured, not quite catching the drift of his remarks.

"It's seeing things in shades, acting in shades of shades. Life made a perfect art. . . ."

"Oh, I see. . . ."

"The French know better than any other people the art of living. And even when the barbarous foreigner flings coin at him, the decorous Frenchman, be he no more than a waiter, resents the violation of the human balance. D'you know what happened the other night at the Restaurant—?" Rennell named one of the most select restaurants of the Right Bank. "An American multi-millionaire was entertaining a party of friends at dinner. In the middle of the meal he called for a *carte de vins*. 'I say, *garçon*,' he said to the *maître d'hôtel*, 'can you tell me the most expensive liqueur on this card?' He was politely informed. 'Have a bottle here at once!' he ordered. It was, of course, a sacrilege to serve liqueur between courses. After a long deliberate delay the bottle came. And do you know what happened? They gulped down the whole bottle then and there! Gulped it down, mind you, as you might a whisky and soda. Even an Englishman doesn't do that. And you should have seen the waiters fume. 'The pigs! The pigs!' they said to one another. . . ."

"My, wasn't that awful?" agreed Mrs. Prescott.

"That's the critical spirit in life and in art, for which

France is justly famous. And in this sense, that handsome girl who brought us our drinks is a true daughter of France!"

At the word "daughter" Mrs. Prescott's thoughts once more unhappily reverted to Ethel and the object of her own mission to this place.

Rennell observed her hesitation and read her thoughts. "I think you had something to tell me," he said.

"Yes," she replied, and bluntly launched into the story of her life.

I I

She was descended from one of the oldest Colonial families in New England. On her father's side she was an Armstrong, on her mother's a Selden. That meant something in New England, where to be born an Armstrong was to be given initial advantages in life only outweighed by the advantages of being born a Selden. The Selden blood was a shade bluer than the Armstrong, but what its particular advantages were she failed to see, except that it gave her mother an opportunity, which she in nowise neglected, of constantly reminding her husband what a condescension on her part it had been to marry him; until the poor man heartfully wished she had been less condescending and honored some one more worthy of her precious Selden blood. He was a Socratic sort of man and bore the trials of being married to a Selden patiently. Fortunately for him, New England Xantippes, by custom, limited their criticism of their husbands to oral exhibitions and avoided the more drastic means employed by the Athenian matron to put her husband to shame.

Whatever their differences in other respects, the Armstrongs laid a great deal of store by their only child, whom they had named Mary, and each attributed the apparent virtues of the charming girl to their own branch of the family and the less desirable qualities—discovered, to be sure, only in irate moments—to the other. The husband was driven to this only in self-defense.

In the divided household Mary grew up, a charming girl to all appearances, and when the time came she married a Prescott, much to Mr. Armstrong's joy and Mrs. Armstrong's disgust. For a Prescott—at all events, this particular Mr. Prescott—was not as good as a Selden, not even as good as an Armstrong. His ancestors had come over from England in the nineteenth century, instead of the seventeenth; and on a steamer instead of a sail-boat. That had been a great mistake; it made all the difference.

Thomas Prescott was a prosperous young broker in Wall Street, and generous to a fault. He bought his bride a lovely old house of her own choosing in the Connecticut hills and to give it the atmosphere to which she had been accustomed, he filled it full of fine antiques. He left her there reveling among them, while daily he commuted to New York to carry on his business. It was nice having a house full of antiques, especially at first, while she was becoming acquainted with them and while she was carrying Ethel. But antiques, even the best of them, are only antiques; and the time came when, in the absence of living interests, the very sight of the beautiful old things palled intolerably. In the hours between the husband's departure at eight in the morning and his return at seven at night there was little or nothing to do, a capable servant attended to all the work of the house, and she spent many daylight hours moving like a wraith from room to room or pressing her face against the window looking down the long elm-lined street watching cars and people go by.

Her husband always was very kind to her. Scarcely a day passed but that he brought back with him some gewgaw or knickknack and now and then something of substantial value such as a fur coat or a modish frock or a piece of jewelry, things to please any woman. She always showed delight fitting to the occasion, only to put the objects away and resume her daily stand at the window. What did she hope to see as she scanned the sidewalks or peered down the long straight street? There was wistfulness in her gaze, and inexpressible longing, while sometimes a wild hope, born of day-dreaming, sprang in her heart, a hope that presently something incredible would happen, some unlooked-for miracle, which would change the current of her life. It was as if she were not living in reality but in some impossible dream, in some horrible state evoked by evil genii, and presto!—she would suddenly awake and, in the twinkling of an eye, find everything different!

With Ethel growing up, she found occupation for part of the time. But in the idle hours the window automatically drew her, lured her with irresistible fascination hard to explain, and she kept on looking out, with the same vague expectancy of something, she knew not what. Now and then she caught sight of a neighbor across the street, a newly married matron looking out of the window. And she found herself wondering as to whether she too were waiting for something which did not and would not appear. She conceived a sympathetic interest in the stranger and often felt a strange impulse to cross the street and embrace the young pretty woman who had such a wistful face and longing eyes. It was all madness, of course. She was afraid she was going mad, and she wanted to run out of the house and run and run and run, and scream and scream and scream. In the evening she felt better again, as was often the way with nervous people, but even her good-natured, obtuse husband began to feel that something was wrong. What could be wrong? He was a good husband to her, and she wanted nothing. He worked hard all day for her good and Ethel's, and he treated them worshipfully as if they were Queen and Princess. And he gave them things. And still more things. He loved giving them things and to watch their eyes light up ecstatically when the gift was particularly desirable. He worked and lived for his family. It was his life. If you took that from him, then he had nothing. He was not so very uncommon a type of American.

"What can I do for you, Mary?" he asked one day. "I mean something that I haven't already done. Is there anything you want particularly that I can bring from town?"

"No, there's nothing you can give me, Tom," she said quite truthfully.

"But you seem unhappy," he persisted. "I'm sure there's something you want...."

"Yes, there is!" she said finally.

"What?" he asked eagerly.

"I don't know."

This sort of thing exasperated both of them. She was annoyed because he asked her what she wanted instead of giving it to her, and he because he was good to her and was willing to give her anything within reason if only she'd tell him what.

Couldn't he see she wanted a different kind of life? What was the good of telling him? He wouldn't understand. He hadn't any conception of a different life, the life she wanted. She scarcely had one herself. Only she knew, felt it in the marrow of her bones, that there was a different kind of life somewhere, perhaps far, far beyond the visible boundaries ... perhaps outside her state, perhaps outside America ... a life dreamt about or read about in books. A vision of Europe hovered before her, a smiling wraith promising wonders.

"I don't know ..." she always answered his question doggedly. But once, only once, she departed from the routine answer. She said: "Take me to Naples! Let me lie on a luxurious bed in the Hotel Excelsior, or sit on the balcony watching the lovely harbor in the sun and with the smoke of Vesuvius rising against the blue sky!"

"Heavens, child! Where did you get such ideas? Read about them in novels, I suppose!"

"Perhaps ..." she answered, and did not mention the subject again.

Then she made up her mind to something: her daughter must not make the mistake of leading her kind of life. At all costs, she must save Ethel from that dire devastating thing. She spent many wakeful days and sleepless nights in trying to think out ways and means to accomplish this. At last she determined on a course of action. As a preliminary, she sent Ethel to a boarding school in which there was a preponderance of courses in eurhythmics, deportment and art instruction. She had reasoned well. Art, she scented with unerring in-

stinct, in its essence expressed the world of her heart's
desire. Behind its veil of beauty she thought she detected palpitating dancing shadows and heard music
calling for votaries to join. Could her daughter resist
their siren-like insistence?

And in recounting to the sympathetic Rennell these
facts of her earlier existence she remembered, with singular vividness, the terrifying dream she had had, sym-
bolic of this period of her life.

It happened on the night after she had seen Ethel,
then a charming girl of sixteen, safely entrained for
boarding school. She dreamt that she was suddenly shot
up in an elevator to a large hexagonal room. Each wall
had a door. There were six doors in all. And she felt as
if she were called upon to make a terrible decision. One
of the doors contained behind it what she wanted.
"Knock and it shall be opened," a voice whispered.
And in palpable silence she was left alone there to make
the decision. Which door? She felt with a fearful certainty the presence of evil spirits behind the closed
doors. The moments passed by slowly, ponderously. She
felt their terrible weight on her frail shoulders. Her
heart beat with great hammer beats, her throat was
parched, in her soul's pain she wanted to cry out but
couldn't utter a sound. With the frozen terror of one
paralyzed she watched the doors slowly open a chink,
and out of the darkness of the unlighted chambers she

thought she saw leering eyes peer out. Something terrible was impending, she knew with that deadly certainty one feels on the brink of a catastrophe. Suddenly, out of nowhere, there appeared a man's figure. His back was turned to her, but by its contours she knew him to be her husband, Tom. Slowly he turned, and showed his face to her, and, horror of horrors!—it was amorphous. Two expressionless eyes alone showed in that featureless face, and they stared at her with an uncomprehending steady stare. She gave a shriek, swooned, and felt herself falling, falling. . . . She awoke, bathed in perspiration and heard Tom at her side ask solicitously, "What's the matter, dear?" while his hands gently stroked her forehead. Involuntarily, hardly knowing why, she shrank from him, saying, "What a horrid dream!" But, in response to his question, she refused to divulge what she had dreamt.

The relation between husband and wife grew increasingly strained, and there was no telling what might not have happened had not the stirring events of August, 1914, broken in upon them, lending some vicarious excitement to their meager lives. With America's entry into the war, Tom tried to enlist, but was rejected because of his eyes, and in the following year, a healthy, able-bodied man, he died in the "flu" epidemic. The fault for this was hers, she was willing to admit; for the poor man, deprived of his last illusion as to his family life, the only life he knew, had lost all will to live and made no resistance to the ravages of the disease. Tom's death left Mrs. Prescott free, with a moderate income, to do as she pleased. She was now a well-preserved woman of forty, her daughter a lovely eager girl of nineteen with life before her. The world had by now decided that women should enjoy the same rights and privileges as men, and things looked propitious.

Long repressed, she was now in her element. For she was by nature—it was a bitter thing to confess—something of a "managing woman," and her particular tragedy had been that too long she had had nothing to manage. Now she suddenly felt her wings; the sensation of newly found freedom, the perception of another world, immense and unexplored, the prospect of seeing this world and of living in it, gave her a fresh lease on life.

And there was another thing. She had a life to shape, her daughter's; the thought gave her unaccountable deep pleasure. It was a source, too, of energy and determination. What a reservoir of life there was in her waiting to be used and directed into proper channels! Like a general, she began plotting a campaign, the conquest of a world glimpsed as yet from afar; and the chief weapon of the promised conquest was her charming daughter, whom she must proceed in making still more charming. She would use her daughter as a potter uses his clay or as a sculptor his marble in fashioning a work fair to

see. It was, after all, for her daughter's good, for her
daughter's happiness. And Ethel would live to thank her
for it. As for herself, she would live in contemplation of
her daughter's happiness, in the serene consciousness of
having been its instrument. And as she had been denied
an opportunity of having the "right sort of life" herself,
she would see to it that her daughter had it; and she
would, as the saying goes, "live in her daughter."

III

While Mrs. Prescott was planning on a course of action which would open the doors of new life for herself and her daughter, her plans, to her dismay, suffered an unexpected hitch. A young man—moreover, a very nice young man—appeared on the scene, and it was clear that for a while he would fill the chief place in the picture for Ethel.

John Whitney was fresh from college and was about to enter his father's prosperous New York house. He had a broad, good-natured face, which promised to grow more good-natured as it mellowed with the years; there was something very young, very boyish in his blue eyes, which seemed always on the verge of smiling but didn't, as if too shy in the presence of a girl; and his six-foot frame, which had not yet filled in, gave indications of being strong and lithe, of affording ample protection to a girl of his choice; his voice, which had a slight New England twang, softened by the Harvard inflection, bespoke a natural kindness and restraint and had a bare touch of tenderness, almost feminine.

"Isn't he tall, mother?" was Ethel's comment after his first visit. "And isn't he nicely built? And hasn't he nice eyes? And isn't he altogether a really nice young man?"

"Yes, he's six feet at least, and every inch a nice young man!" said her mother, laughing at her daughter's innocent encomium, and giving the last words a peculiar intonation, full of shades of meaning.

"You don't like him, I see!" said Ethel, laughing in her turn. She was always frank with her mother, which gave their relation a sense of chumminess.

"What ever gave you that idea?" her mother protested. "You know what I mean!"

"Yes, I do. You mean that being nice is not nice at all. You don't think he's a moron?"

"How can you say such a thing?" said her mother quite earnestly. "I think he's very nice, indeed. He reminds me of your father when he first fell in love with me. Almost the image of him, I should say! In the way he looks, and particularly in the way he acts. It's quite undefinable, almost uncanny!"

"Were you very much in love with father when you first met?"

"Very. . . ."

"Yet you didn't get on very well later?"

"No. . . ."

"Did father demand too much from you?"

"Not enough. . . . That was the trouble. He didn't demand enough of himself, either."

"Father was good?"

"Terribly good. . . . It would have been better if he weren't so good."

"What do you mean?"

"He was terribly kind. He was always bringing me things."

"That must have been nice."

At the reiteration of the word, "nice," Mrs. Prescott laughed.

"You always laugh when I use that word," said Ethel; for the peculiar circumstance did not go by her unnoticed. "Why do you? I always have the feeling that you mock at it!"

"Not really," her mother made haste to say. "What I mean is, that he brought me nothing I really terribly wanted!"

"What's that?"

"We will talk about it one day."

"Still, it's terribly nice having a man bring one

things! It must show that he thinks of you always, and that he loves you!"

Ethel looked perplexed. Wistfulness crept into her eyes, as she dropped her gaze upon the lovely Bokhara rug, one of the numerous gifts of her father to her mother. She loved beautiful things, and she could go into raptures over soft fine textures. Her slender virginal form looked seductive curled up in the big chair, and her long curling lashes and her almost transparent lids under broad curving eye-brows which might have been drawn by the pencil of a great artist gave her that ultimate touch of loveliness which touched the heart of the mother and only made her the more determined that this loveliness should not be wasted on an unworthy lover who, as husband, might make her daughter's existence as tedious as her own.

"My dear child!" she exclaimed, with real tenderness. "You are almost too young to understand. There are thousands of women in this world who have everything that rich husbands can give them, and who are yet unhappy. . . . I don't want you to make a ghastly mistake in life!"

Ethel's look of perplexity grew more intense, as she eyed her mother with just a trace of suspicion in her eyes. Her mother saw this look, and made haste to say:

"Don't think, my dear child, that I want to keep you

from nice young men. You're a young girl, and it's natural for you to want to meet young men. . . ."

"I dream of them. . . ."

"Quite so. And so did I when I was about your age. I married the first man that wanted me. And I was his first love. . . . But for your own sake, I want you to wait till you've had a little more experience, seen more of the world. I don't want you to fall victim to the first man who makes love to you, and whom you happen to like. I want you to meet many young men and choose from among them. I have great plans for you. And I want my little girl to be very, very happy. . . ."

"I thought first love was always beautiful. All the poets have written so glowingly about it. They say what comes after is never quite the same."

"I thought so too! And I married your father. . . . He brought me things, lots of things. . . ." She laughed, and there was a hysterical note in her laughter. "But, oh, my dear, how I have sometimes wished for. . . ." But she reconsidered, and did not go on.

"What did you wish, what?" Ethel demanded.

"I wished, how often I wished, to put everything in one great pile and set a match to it! To watch it burn would have given me great happiness!"

"No, no, mother, you were going to say something else! You know you were! I could tell it from your face. What did you wish? What?"

"Well, child . . . I wished, instead of bringing me gifts, he'd have beaten me! If only he really loved me at the same time!"

Ethel laughed. "You're a silly mummy! And what a ridiculous notion! I sometimes don't understand you."

But she did not press the matter. For the time being, the subject was dropped.

Mrs. Prescott saw that there was much yet to be done to educate her daughter in the right notions of life, and that it would take a long time to do it. She had, first of all, to eradicate certain boarding-school ideas, and ideas borrowed from falsely romantic books. She must be patient. She must abide her time. She must match her strength against the strength of any raw young man who dared to think that he was good enough for her daughter. She would, if need be, let any "affair" drift to the penultimate degree, and then—oh, she would find a way! The idea excited her, she saw a possible outlet in it for her boiling energies; her imagination was already working hard as to ways and means of circumventing importunate young men; it lent a zest and a flavor to existence. It was like skating on thin ice, she knew—or playing with fire; for she must outwardly encourage and inwardly destroy; she must accomplish her purpose without arousing the hostility of her child. Everything, if it was to succeed, must come about naturally; Ethel must never know that her mother had meddled.

She saw nothing reprehensible in all this. It did not once strike her that there was anything wrong in it. She saw her goal, and thought it worthy, and did not care what means she used to arrive at it. Young men will venture, and young men must bear their disappointments. It was the law of life. There was a struggle for possession, and the prize went to the strongest. They would see who was stronger, they or she. And who had the most valid claim on an only daughter, a young man of no startling merit, or a mother who wanted to make her daughter a prize worth contending for? Besides— and this was her supreme argument, which she invariably fell back upon at the slightest twinge of conscience —she was fighting for her daughter's happiness, a happiness she herself had missed. Let young Whitney pay court to her daughter! She welcomed it as a diversion, as a taste of experience for her daughter; and she accepted it as a challenge to herself, which she was only too ready to face. There was nothing like putting an idea to the test.

Actually, she saw no danger in this "nice" unsophisticated youth for her "artistic" Ethel. So young Whitney was made welcome by mother as well as by daughter, and so frequent became his visits and so quickly did the acquaintance ripen into intimacy, that it was not long before they called him simply, Jack. Mrs. Prescott could not help noticing that Ethel was happier than she had ever been before, that she no longer fell into those moody spells so common to her before Jack appeared on the scene, and that she always "perked up" at the mere prospect of Jack's coming. Mrs. Prescott attached no undue importance to this. She knew that "girls will be girls," that the devotion of young men was always welcome to them, and that this counter-attraction by no means always led to marriage; not nowadays, at any rate. There were many such interludes in attractive girls' lives. It was their due, she thought; and their attractions merely throve on the multitude of young men's devotions. Then one day comes, and lo!—*the* young man appears, he for whom all the former young men had been as forerunners, as the necessary sacrifices making this supreme conjunction possible; he too had been prepared by numerous girl sacrifices in order that he might meet *the* one girl. Such was the extraordinary theory Mrs. Prescott entertained, and heaven alone knows where she got it. But to use her own homely image: an ax was sharpened by the grindstone, and all these *not quite* worthy young men were merely here to serve as grindstones to charming girls, sharpening them up for the young man yet to come, who could and would appreciate a fine blade.

Did she realize the dangers of her plan, that the finer

the blade the more chance it ran of being refined out of existence or nicked by an uncouth grindstone? She did think of it sometimes, but being determined on a ruthless Napoleonic course she swept all objections aside as being unworthy of her and of the noble goal she entertained. She would, surely, be criminally negligent, if after her own disastrous experience, she allowed its repetition for her daughter. She commended herself for her good intentions.

In the meanwhile, Ethel, unconscious of her mother's ambitious plans for her, found herself more and more drawn towards Jack, whose tenderness awakened reciprocal feelings. How gentle he was, how thoughtful, how considerate! He rarely came without bringing flowers, and always peace, quiet ecstasy, happiness. Her girlish heart fluttered at the sight of him, while to cover up flushes and excitement she always made haste to rearrange the cushions in the big chair ostensibly to make it more comfortable for him, though she could have scarcely made it more comfortable than it already was. Then, seated, they cast overt glances at one another, and these glances were charged with meanings greater than any that ever charged mere words. Eye leapt to eye, spark to spark, their young bodies flamed with feelings of sweet pain held in check. At first they scarcely spoke of love. Was there any need of it? Was there pleasure greater than standing on the brink of momentous words,

words never uttered but lingering in the air and warming it with a delicious warmth which diffused itself through their bodies and spoke with a strange eloquence in their blood?

Then there were their walks together over the Litchfield hills, and through the pine woods, and up and down country lanes, arm in arm, keeping step with one another as if they were one body—did they not feel as one body? And, unwatched, their love grew as freely and as naturally as the field flowers they saw in their seasons. There was the trailing arbutus they admired together in April sweeping the meadows with their all-covering ardent pink; there were the gentle violets which they picked in May while furtively he glanced at the graceful bend of her slender virginal body and she at his stalwart muscular frame lithe for all its bigness; there were the June roses, a symbol of the maturing of the season and of their as yet unspoken love. And moved by the sight of profuse roses, the sap of youth overflowed in them, and the words, long hovering, came naturally and softly to his lips:

"Ethel, I love you!"

Though she had been long expecting these words, yet, when they came, they overwhelmed her, and she fell back against him as if she were going to swoon, while his arm encircled her and held her, and she was fainting with happiness. He kissed her, and she did not resist. He felt her trembling, while her nervous hands clutched his shoulders. This was sweet beyond all anticipation; as one column they reeled, as if drunken, and happy as in a dream.

"I love you! Oh, how I love you!" she murmured at last. "And yet I don't know. . . . I don't know. . . ."

"You don't know what?" he asked, perplexed, while the tense arm holding her relaxed a little.

"Let's sit down on that stone," she said.

An arm around each other's waist, they walked to the stone, and sat down. He waited for her to speak.

"You know I love you. . . . You must have known it a long time. . . ."

He nodded in the affirmative.

"We are happy now," she went on. "But shall we always be happy?"

"Why shouldn't we be?" he asked, his perplexed look returning. "We were made for one another!"

"I know . . . I know. . . . But that's what father said to mother, when they first fell in love with one another. . . ."

"What of that?" His perplexity increased.

"What of that?" she echoed him. "They were happy only at the beginning."

"Oh, that!" he answered with the assurance of youth. "Don't let that worry you. I know I shall always love you!"

"But shall I always love you?" she asked, smiling, pressing his hand hard.

"Oh, forgive me!" he said. "It was selfish of me to speak of myself first. But why shouldn't you be happy? I know I shall love you always, and I think you will always love me. I shall do everything I can to make you love me, keep you in love with me!"

"I know . . . I know . . ." she went on murmuring, half certain, half dubious.

"You will find me always devoted to you!" he pleaded. "How indeed can I be otherwise? . . . I shall shower you with attentions . . . I shall bring you flowers . . . I shall bring you . . ."

"Don't! Please don't!" she cried, half in horror, recoiling from him, and putting her hand over his mouth to keep him from speaking.

"Now, what have I done?" he asked, half guiltily, yet unaware of the nature of his guilt.

"Don't you see," she said. "You mustn't say such things, unless you want to scare me away. If I marry you, I shan't marry you for things! I won't! So there! I don't want things. Father gave mother ever so many things, and yet she wasn't happy. Many things made her unhappy, and she was like one lost among them. . . . You don't understand?" She looked closely into his eyes, as if she wanted to ferret some deep secret out of his soul. "I see you don't understand. A woman may like things, but it isn't things that make her happy. Father was so devoted to mother, yet . . ."

She paused, and clung more tightly to him than before. It was as if she were clinging desperately to the hope that he was different from her father, and that he had the integrity in him to hold her love more securely than her father had held her mother's. She suddenly drew away from him, and again gave his eyes the most searching scrutiny.

"Jack dear! Are you angry?" she said, with something like despair in her voice. "If ever I am wicked, you must beat me!"

"Beat you? Why should I beat you?" He smiled the tenderest of smiles. "A gentleman doesn't usually beat a lady, does he? And certainly not the lady he's in love with. I shall never beat you," he said, with decision.

"If you're really in love with a woman, you would!" she said, this time good-naturedly. "All women rather like it, you know!"

"Really? I don't believe it. . . . You seem serious, yet I don't understand it at all. . . . It's a queer way of showing one's love, I must admit. . . . And I shouldn't think any sensible woman would like it either!"

"Much you know about women, Jack! And there's no such thing as a sensible woman. I'll do all I can to exasperate you when we're married. See if I don't! . . .

Anyhow, you're a dear!" And spontaneously she flung her arms about his neck.

Jack could not make head or tail of such things; they were beyond him; but somehow, inwardly, he felt pleased. She must indeed love him if she were willing to stand a beating at his hands. It made him feel master of her, a pleasant feeling for a man in love.

Ethel returned to the house her face all flushed and with a strange look in her eyes. Instinctively her mother knew what had happened. A reminiscence flooded her mind and body. Had she not herself many years ago returned from a walk, her face flushed in the same fashion, and with that strange ecstatic look in her eyes of a girl who, for the first time, heard a tender avowal from a man's lips? She was frankly astonished. She had not expected the dénouement so quickly. But she gave no hint to the others of her knowledge.

No word was exchanged between mother and daughter until Jack bade them good-night. But Ethel was not a girl to keep so portentous a secret from her mother.

"Mother, Jack and I are engaged," she announced simply.

"I hope you'll be happy," said the older woman, quietly.

Ethel raised her eyes in astonishment. She had expected protests, reproaches, and here her mother actually seemed *almost* glad. "I thought you might be angry," she said.

"Why should I, my darling? All I desire is your happiness. And if Jack can give it to you, why should I object?"

"You darling mummy!" And Ethel flung her arms around her mother's neck. "He's really awfully nice, mummy!"

Her mother, smiling, disengaged herself from the embrace. "I only want to ask you one thing, my dear!"

"And what's that, mother?"

"You're still very young, you know. Don't rush into marriage. Wait a little! Let Jack wait a little!"

"Of course, mother! Jack doesn't intend to marry me until he can support me properly. And as you know, he's only just beginning. His father's rich, but he expects his son to start at the bottom!"

"That's the good old-fashioned Yankee way!" said her mother, with evident approval, hiding the still greater inward satisfaction she felt at this information. She casually added: "That's the way Tom started. And Tom made good!"

Ethel was happier than she had ever felt before. To have been proposed to by Jack and won her mother's sanction for their love was a greater piece of fortune than she could have anticipated on the same day. Only later, in the quiet hours of the night—happy sleepless night, with images of Jack passing and repassing—she for an instant wondered why her mother mentioned her father in just that way, for she knew her mother did not always respect those who "made good." In her happiness, however, she quickly dismissed the matter from her mind, and her girlish fancies returned to the more pleasant contemplation of the intruding figure of her beloved.

At the same time her mother was passing a sleepless night in her room. The rapid turn in developments had upset her calculations, and made her problem more difficult. She knew it to be her duty to undermine the engagement without forfeiting Ethel's confidence. She must be careful, must handle the situation gingerly, must use every device—every stratagem—to circumvent the marriage, must use every subtle insinuation to bring about the ultimate rupture; and throughout it all, her hand must remain unsuspected, invisible.

There was an instant when qualms seized her. To all appearances, her daughter was happy; was it not possible that this happiness, if let alone, would prove lasting? But she cast this possibility from her as a consideration unworthy of her exalted purpose. For, after all, she was not trying to destroy her daughter's happiness, but to intensify its quality. And she could not give up the dream of making her daughter happy in the manner she herself desired to be happy if she had her life to live all over again. It was hard to give this up, she would not give it up. Jack, to be sure, was a nice boy, even an awfully nice boy, as Ethel had said. Well, that being the case, he would swallow his disappointment, grieve for a little while, and then find for himself, as many a man before him had done, a nice girl, even an awfully nice girl. She wished Jack no harm, but she was a mother, and she must protect her daughter at all costs. And with this thought, her courage returned to her, and her mind went wandering to ways and means of accomplishing her noble purpose.

The next day Jack came as usual, and he and Mrs. Prescott had a talk; a very satisfactory one to Jack. For she accepted him as her daughter's future husband, with the sole proviso that he wait a little before rushing Ethel to the altar.

"Ethel is so very young, you know," she repeated almost the same words she had used to Ethel. "And waiting can do no harm, it can only do good."

Jack agreed with her in every particular, and assured her that he did not intend rushing matters, all the more as, despite his father's wealth, he had his way to make and was not yet in a position to make his wife's home fitting to her charm and position.

"I told you mother was a dear," said Ethel, in her mother's presence.

"She certainly is," agreed Jack.

The lovers, arm in arm, departed to the woods, perfectly happy.

Mrs. Prescott smiled benignly after them. For an instant her qualms returned to her, but as during the night she swept them aside. What are qualms to a woman with a fixed idea and a long-deliberated plan? She would yet make Ethel the happiest girl in the world, and she, her mother, would yet bask in the rays of her daughter's happiness.

"Seeing you together," she said to Ethel a few days later, "is almost as if Tom were again paying court to me. We were so happy together in those days! . . ." And, observing a curious look in her daughter's eyes, she spontaneously added: "I do want to see my little daughter the happiest little girl in the world!"

"We want you to live with us, mother. We three shall be the happiest family anywhere. Jack likes you a lot!"

Mrs. Prescott received this statement with apparent satisfaction. "I am glad," she said. "Funny, but that's what Tom said to my mother!"

Ethel laughed. It seemed such a funny thing for her mother to say. But her mother had said it in such a naïve, almost child-like way that Ethel straightway embraced her, and said: "You're a dear! You are, really!"

The days passed into weeks, the weeks into months; Mrs. Prescott made time the basis of her strategy. She knew her daughter to be romantic, therefore impatient.

It was good policy to prolong the engagement. With the autumn, Jack entered his father's firm, and was able to come only at week-ends, and now and then in the middle of the week. With this readjustment, Ethel's former fits of moodiness returned, and she found in her mother a ready sympathizer.

"You now see, my dear," her mother would say, looking out upon the sear landscape, in which lovely reds were beginning to mingle with green-tawny foliage, "what my own life has been. This is how I used to stand in the old days when your father was still alive. He would go to town to his work, while I would stay here all alone and wait . . . and wait. . . ."

And she would lapse into silence, and let her sad eyes, dreamy with reminiscence, search the remote distance down and beyond the long elm-lined street. She knew what she was doing; knew that the seed of discontent she had sown in her daughter's heart would thrive best in the long autumn and the still longer winter silences, and, given time, would bear abundantly the fruit she so ardently desired. And Ethel would thank her for it.

Jack, naïve and optimistic, unsuspicious of the devious workings of men and women's minds, did not know how to account for the mixed receptions with which he was greeted week-ends at Biddlebury.

Ethel appeared, as before, happy, oh, so happy, to see him; yet he could scarcely help observing inexplicable moments when Ethel appeared to withdraw within herself, to hold back something he knew not what. It troubled him deeply, though he did not attach ultimate importance to the circumstance; all the more as these moments were interspersed with intense moments of almost hysterical abandon on Ethel's part, leaving him in no doubt of her love for him. He was a mere boy, and he accepted these extremes of coolness and warmth as the emotional balances by which the delicious female sex was governed, and he congratulated himself upon the prospective acquisition of a girl who, whatever faults she had—not that he could see any—would furnish him with that rapture which he could not help learning was denied to so many of his countrymen. But once or twice Ethel startled him, almost frightened him, by breaking from his embrace, with the almost indignant fiery words, fiercely spoken:

"If you really loved me, Jack, you'd take me away from here! To-day! At once!"

He, turning a hurt expression upon her, like one wounded without knowing how or why, would ask gently:

"What's the trouble, my dear?"

But she, ignoring his question, ignoring his obvious pain, would, by way of response, cry with something like despair:

"I can't stand it! I can't stand it!"

"Can't stand what?"

But she would persist:

"If you really loved me, Jack, you'd take me away from here, from mother, from everybody!"

"But I do love you! Wait a little, my dear! How can I take you away until I can give you a proper home?"

"It's always wait, wait, wait! I'm tired of waiting! I don't want a proper home! I don't want things! I want life! Life!"

Such outbursts disturbed him, made him conscious of his limitations. What was life, anyhow? He offered her what any decent man was supposed to offer the woman of his choice: shelter, food, protection, devotion, the care of her babes to come: everything embraced within the word Love. What was it she wanted? And he had heard the word "Life" used among his male companions as if it meant something quite extraneous to these things, something almost improper. He could not for an instant entertain the thought that such a sweet innocent girl could want anything improper. But this did not help matters any, and the increasing frequency of her cool-nesses and fierce outbursts hurt him as much as they mystified and disturbed him. Momentary suspicions crossed his unusually unsuspicious mind of Ethel's mother being at the bottom of it all. But he could not be sure of it; she was so friendly, so constantly welcoming. Once in her presence, he dismissed his suspicions as unworthy, and attributed his difficulties to his own lack somewhere.

And then he made his supreme mistake. Not knowing what else to do, he increased his devotions, began to bring Ethel more and more things: flowers and all manner of gifts.

"How like your father!" Mrs. Prescott would say, with an innocent air, and sometimes with amusement.

And Ethel no longer took the trouble to make a response.

Then, gradually, Mrs. Prescott desisted.

One day she was reading the local newspaper when, her eyes alighting on an item in the society column, she exclaimed:

"Goodness gracious, Ethel! Do you remember Jane Kilmer?"

"Yes, mother."

"Well, you remember what a little frump she was, and how no one would look at her!"

"I can't say she was much to look at," admitted Ethel, who more charitably added: "But I liked Jane. She was a good sort!"

"Well, as you know, she went abroad with her mother, and went to art school in Paris."

"Well?"

"Well, you wouldn't believe it, my dear! But she's apparently blossomed out. She's right in the swim, and she's going to marry the famous English artist, Mr. Lionel Manderville! Who'd have believed it?"

"It's rather wonderful, isn't it?" said Ethel, her eyes lighting up. "I'm glad for her. She must have come on! They say Europe develops people!"

Her mother did not say anything, but a spark of joy in her heart cheered her whole being. She felt here was a trump card, and that it had won.

One morning, about a fortnight later, she said fervently:

"You know, I think we're drifting into a groove, my dear! What do you say if we go to New York to-day and engage passage on the *Berengaria?* I see it sails a week from to-day!"

"That would be simply wonderful, mother!" cried Ethel, clapping her hands. Then, suddenly growing grave, she asked: "What about Jack? It would be hard on him!"

"Oh, Jack!" her mother replied sympathetically. "Of course! But that's quite all right, I'm sure. You need a change, you know, and Jack loves you too much to want to deny you anything. And, anyhow, if he loves you, he will come after you. It's one way of finding out how much a man loves a girl. Or if you find you miss Jack too much, what's to hinder us from coming back? Not for the world would I have my little girl think that I stand in her way!"

"What a generous mummy you are!" exclaimed Ethel warmly, while her mother smiled the smile of one who was conscious of conferring a largesse. But there was an inward meaning to her smile.

Thus the matter was settled. A week later, mother and daughter left for France, leaving Jack behind to console himself as best he could.

For some months letters went back and forth across the Atlantic, full of passionate bereavement on Jack's part, of palpably cooling regret on Ethel's, until the correspondence ceased altogether. Jack was forgotten, left to bemoan the lot of the luckless lover, while Ethel, abetted by her mother, found new exciting interests to occupy her time and mind.

Biddlebury, Connecticut, and the little white house, were also forgotten in the distractions of the gay city.

I V

The new world into which Mrs. Prescott and her daughter were suddenly plunged was not long in revealing its delights to them. The Great War had been over for two years, the women of the American colony seethed with the joy of newly found freedom, with the joys of emancipated sex no longer bound by old conventions. They settled in a little flat on the Left Bank. Ethel went to art school and made many friends, especially among the male sex, who found her singularly charming. Her naïveté and spontaneity—and something of the quality of Daisy Miller—appealed to their appetites not a little jaded by the War and blasé companions. She enjoyed being the object of infatuation, and her discovery of her peculiar power of attracting men delighted her and, scarcely less, her doting mother.

Mrs. Prescott was not a little delighted on her own account. Men did not leave her out of their attentions and once or twice she suffered the not unpleasant suspicion that they preferred her to her daughter. Mother and daughter good-naturedly chided one another about their conquests. Each in her own way bloomed in the amorous Parisian sun. After her long hunger, in austere Biddlebury, for thrilling experience Mrs. Prescott sometimes acted rather over-eagerly, courting in consequence, without deserving it, the appellation of "wanton." She marveled at the attractiveness of Parisian widows and, taking a leaf out of their book, affected black attire which set off her fair hair and gave her figure an almost girlish slenderness.

She played with the idea of freedom and, while allowing herself to philander with men, she shirked the ultimate experience she so intensely desired; her ample store of inhibitions acting as so much ballast against her being carried off her feet. And as each disgruntled cavalier withdrew from pursuit of the reluctant widow she was left boasting of still another triumph, insinuating on occasion to her confidants what a serious affair it had been and how sorry she had been to upset the poor fellow. She could scarcely be blamed for so innocent a diversion. It amused her mightily, and it was so delightful to appear wicked. And it did no one any particular harm.

It was different with Ethel who, ardent with youth, took her new life seriously. Young men attracted her, took on the aura of mystery; she grasped the essential fact: if life was to be lived to the full, this mystery must be solved. And she proceeded to fall in love. Jan Petchor-ski, a young romantic-looking Pole with long black locks under a broad-brimmed black hat and mischievous sparkling dark eyes took her fancy; and he, for his part, was not blind to the patent attractions of this spirited American girl. He was a promising artist of one of the newer schools and his gifts, such as they were, were be-ginning to be appreciated in that small but select world which regarded Rembrandt and Velasquez as passé and no art possibly great which could be understood. In his color compositions he utilized such things as real shoe buttons, cigarette stubs and burnt match sticks, and even frayed lace from women's discarded undergar-ments; indeed anything that came to hand; and equally ultra-modern critics and friends came and applauded. The public was amused. Every one was satisfied, and no harm was done.

"I'm a realist," Jan intelligently declared. "I paint life as I see it. And what is life but a conglomeration of disjointed fragments? If I choose to use shoe-buttons for eyes it's because I see human beings that way. You must admit that if they had other kind of eyes they'd appre-ciate my art!"

Such an argument appeared unanswerable.

Strangely enough, in actual life, Jan Petchorski was a romantic. He was something of a daredevil, and his war experiences in the Foreign Legion would in themselves have filled a book. Ethel was captivated and accepted his attentions; and Mrs. Prescott beamed on them both. He became a regular visitor at their apartment, and he and Ethel daily repaired to a café, too often accompanied by Mrs. Prescott. Now and then they were joined by Jan's friends, and there was much talk. And what talk! Jan had an excellent command of English, but he often broke into French or Polish. Because she could not understand Mrs. Prescott tacitly beamed all the more. Foreign tongues which she did not understand had a peculiar attraction for her; she could hardly have explained why. As for Ethel, she understood French perfectly, though she spoke it hesitatingly. She was a good listener, and she hung on Jan's words, which were quite unlike the words of any other man. Not alone the words but the manner in which he spoke them. It was very effective with women. Very.

The time inevitably came when Jan accomplished his purpose. . . . Yes, and Mrs. Prescott had to admit that she had had a hand in it. Hadn't she long enough preached to her daughter about the need of women's freedom, about the hateful double standard of morality, one for men and another for women, and how the time

had come for women to conduct their lives in any manner they saw fit just as the men did? "What's wild oats
for the gander is wild oats for the goose!" was her way
of putting it. Ethel indeed had been at first inclined to
disagree with this dictum, but rising to the occasion she
succumbed to the more convincing argument of passion,
and became Jan's acknowledged mistress.

When apprised of it a day or two afterwards, her
mother was stunned and for some minutes said nothing.
However prepared her mind was to accept theoretically
the emancipation of women, however ready she was to
applaud emancipated women practicing the tenets of
their new faith, to see her own daughter precipitate herself into a state which she had been taught to call "living
in sin" came something in the nature of a shock. How
difficult it was to reconcile one's fettered emotions with
the independence of one's thought! And in the face of
the *fait accompli*, she was assailed by scruples. Had she
done right by her daughter? If, at least, the man she had
chosen had been some outstanding celebrity, some one
worthy of Ethel . . . but Jan Petchorski! After all, who
was Jan? She had a suspicion of there being Jewish blood
in his veins. The spirit of the Daughters of the American
Revolution and of the Colonial Dames had unexpectedly
come to life, taunting her.

She thought quickly. She had to. Paramount in her
mind was the thought that, come what may, she must not

lose her daughter's confidence. She had foreseen the possibility of what had happened (not with Jan, of course),
and was, in a measure, prepared for it. So, after a short
silence, she said:

"That's quite all right, my dear. Only don't have a
baby, please!"

"Jan has seen to that," she answered, quietly. "He
doesn't want any squalling babies either!"

Mrs. Prescott swallowed hard, and patted her "dear
little girl's" head.

Later, in the reaction, inexplicably to herself, she
reveled in the thought of her daughter's adventure. She
wouldn't have done differently herself if she were only
young and weren't weighed down with so many puritanic
inhibitions. She came to look upon the matter with as-
tonishing equanimity. Jan was a gay, virile, intellectual
animal, and he made Ethel happy—what more could she
ask? We were but a short time on this earth, and happiness was the end of life—let the dear young things enjoy themselves! After all, that was what she had wanted,
what she had so long preached. Vividly she recalled her
own lack in the days in which she had stood, her face
pressed longingly against the window, in that little white
house in the Connecticut hills. Here was romance at last!
Mentally she lived her daughter's experience, vicariously
losing herself in the life she had wanted and never had.
She beamed on Jan and Ethel. . . . But passing from re-

action to reaction, moments of doubt reasserted themselves, and she suffered the agony of the damned. Tears would come to her eyes, and she felt miserable enough to want to die.

What was the use of thinking? Regretting? There was no getting a girl's virtue back. You might as well blow a feather to the winds and expect it to come back!

And, again, she thought self-consolingly, there were men who paid attention to her too. If only she could overcome her physical scruples, alas too firm-rooted, sufficiently to abandon herself to one of these creatures called men! Urged by mentally stimulated desire, she egged them on, and it pleased her to see them court her favor. But when it "came to the scratch," she couldn't, simply couldn't! "The pigs! The pigs!" she would say to herself. "That's all they want, to see how much they can get out of a woman! How much they can shame her! And when they've gotten what they wanted, they—" But she was too wroth, too resentful, to finish her sentence, and she would cry herself to sleep.

Thus life went on, with—for Mrs. Prescott—alternating moods of beaming, doubting, resenting, raging, weeping; while Ethel, unmindful of these changing moods of her mother's, went on enjoying the embraces of her lover as if it were the one thing that mattered.

But everything has an end, and there was an end as well to Ethel's happiness. After three months Jan

showed some signs of cooling, but it was scarcely anticipated that the end was so near. One day he failed to
appear for his appointment at the Prescott flat, and as
this had not happened before, Ethel, thinking he was ill,
hurried to his apartment in rue des Ecoles, and rushed
in breathless upon the concierge.

"Didn't you know?" said the placid, stolid-looking
woman, standing with her arms akimbo and amiably
contemplating the look of fear on the perturbed girl's
face. "Monsieur left this morning!"

"Left? You mean for good?" She trembled. There was
consternation in her voice.

"Yes, madame. . . ."

"But—" She struggled for words. "For where?" she
managed to ask.

"Mon Dieu! How should I know?"

"He didn't leave a note—or anything?" Her desperation was evident.

"I don't think so. Perhaps my husband knows," answered the redoubtable female, suddenly softening. She
wasn't fond of foreigners, and especially of those arro-
gant Americans; but Ethel looked so distraught that,
surmising the nature of her plight, she found herself
overcoming her scruples and pitying the girl. "Just wait
a moment! I'll ask him. . . . Jules!" she called into the
inner chamber. "Has Monsieur in Number Five left a
note for Madame—"

"Prescott . . ." Ethel prompted her.

A portly good-natured figure appeared in the doorway and, sheepishly grinning, drew an envelope from an inside pocket and delivered it into Ethel's trembling hands.

With nervous haste she tore open the envelope, and her whole demeanor revealed to the watching pair the consternation she felt. The note read:

"Ethel my dear! I'm off for London. Can't say when I'll return. Perhaps never. I thought this was the best way. You will remember that at the beginning you and I had fully discussed the possibility of parting. You said that, man and woman, we were both free to act according to our will and desire. (Your mother too, to judge from her often reiterated opinions, appeared to acquiesce.) You must be aware that my feelings towards you, while in every respect friendly, are not quite what they were; yours may be, I don't know. I think it's best to part while we are still friends, don't you? Anyhow, I've for a long time felt restless and have wanted to see London. Don't try to find me. . . . As always, Jan."

"Don't worry, *cheri*," ventured the concierge, guessing what the trouble was. "He isn't worth it! And Paris is full of young men!"

With tears streaming down her face, Ethel left the staring pair, and hastened home. Mrs. Prescott, appalled, tried to comfort her daughter, but to no avail.

"No, mother. It's no use. I loved him, and I could

have been his slave. Freedom and equality don't interest me any more. Love's all that matters.... D'you think he'll return?"

"Of course he'll return!" cried her mother, snatching at any straw to soothe her daughter. "He can't help it!"

"No, no! He'll not return! I know it! I know it!" And Ethel gave way to a fresh effusion of tears.

She was right. The months passed by, and Jan did not return. Ethel grew increasingly wistful and moody. The wistfulness in her eyes appealed to young men, each of whom thought he could assuage the girl's secret grief. Yes, the concierge had been right. Paris was full of young men. And one or two she thought she could grow fond of. Not of course in the way she had been fond of Jan. ... There was no getting round the fact: once she had overstepped the barriers of convention it was far harder to resist her second romantic impulse. Within six months of Jan's departure she had another lover. Again she was happy, but in a less intense degree than before. The mutability of passion had begun to disturb her. It was the one serious flaw in her affair with Roger Wentworth, an American painter living in the Quarter. At the end of three months Roger grew matter-of-fact, "took her for granted" as it were. This time she took matters into her hands and left him. She was not going to suffer the ignominy of having a man leave her a second time. She was not going to let any one have the chance.

Her mother's attitude had been tolerant and kind. She had not liked Ethel taking up with Roger. At the same time, she put no hindrance in the way. Her daughter was so sad, so unhappy; it had nearly broken her heart. She thought Ethel might do harm to herself. And she welcomed any diversion which might give her daughter a measure of happiness, of forgetfulness.

The affair with Roger, she thought, had served at least one good purpose. Ethel no longer thought of Jan. If not ecstatically happy, she was at all events not unhappy.

In the years to come there was to be a small procession of lovers of varying merit. Ethel did not grow discriminating with the years; perhaps she had grown indifferent, did not care if she kept her lamp trimmed or not. Some young men who might have loved this attractive wistful-eyed girl fought shy as soon as they heard of her "past." And yet, in a curious way, she managed to retain a fresh, even virginal appearance, fascinating to a certain type of men.

"My dear," her mother once ventured to remonstrate with her, "you are living on your capital instead of investing it."

"Why, mother!" retaliated the girl warmly. "You talk as though my charms were a bank account."

"So they are! If you waste them, you have so much the less."

"What a material mind you have!" Ethel chided her. "Besides, you yourself have taught me to live freely. And doesn't that mean spend freely? . . . Not that you've said much about it lately."

This dig had the effect of silencing her mother, who lived in the hope of her daughter coming to her senses. After all, if there was anything in blood. . . . In the meanwhile, with rueful eyes, she watched Ethel dissipate the substance of her charms.

Ethel's position was unenviable. She was, it was true, getting sick of lovers, yet she was sicker without them. Such is force of habit. She was becoming intolerably weary and bored. And she drank rather more than was good for her. She was not unaware of what she was doing, for on returning from a café one evening and surveying herself in a mirror she burst into laughter.

Her mother looked up anxiously. "What's up, Ethel?"

"Nothing, mother. Only I was just thinking, what would dear Jack think of me if he saw me now? Would he like my rouged ruby lips? Would he still think me the pure-as-a-lily darling?"

"Jack? Jack?" Her mother looked quizzically at Ethel. "What are you talking about?"

"Why, mother! Have you forgotten Jack Whitney who came to see me at Biddlebury and wanted to make me his dear little wife? Good old Jack, who hardly thought it proper to kiss me until the clergyman gave him

permission!" And she gave way to another outburst of
laughter.

Mrs. Prescott also laughed, but at the same time
thought hard. She almost wished she were back in that
little white house in the Connecticut hills. Memory of
Jack, she did not know why, gave her an uncomfortable,
strangely poignant feeling of regret. Regret for what?
She suddenly thought of the long hours spent in looking
out of the window down the endless straight elm-lined
street, and the memory shook her out of her depression.
Either way life was hard. There was little choice. She
laughed.

Ethel must have read her mother's thoughts, for she
said sympathetically:

"I know it's hard, mummy dear. I couldn't have stood
it, you know. I mean the life you were forced to live.
Fancy living with a man who left you to look out of the
window all day long. No, I couldn't have stood it! Not
all those years. I'd have shot him ... or myself.... Or
I'd have run away...."

"It wasn't as bad as all that," said Mrs. Prescott,
moved to self-defense. She didn't like being thought a
weak spineless creature.

"And to think," went on Ethel, "that if we hadn't left
Biddlebury when we did, I should have married Jack,
and should have been the same as you were, day after
day, hour after hour, standing at the window, looking

down the street, waiting, watching for something to happen, heavens knows what! . . . No, no. Bad as this is, it is better, far better. . . ." It was clear that Ethel was trying to reassure herself, convince herself of this, and that she sought corroboration from her mother.

But her mother merely said: "I try to think so. I hope so. I don't know. . . ."

"Why, mother!" There was reprimand, reproach, despair in Ethel's voice. And it conveyed the sense of being a cry of distress. Its tone gave the impression of her mother, in this crucial moment, having failed her. "You wouldn't have that life back?" she asked with sudden fierceness, almost harshly, determined it seemed of obtaining an equally fervent answer.

"I don't know . . . I don't know . . ." her mother wailed, her eyes fixed on the floor rug. Then, looking up and seeing tears of consternation in Ethel's eyes, she quickly brightened, and cried: "Of course not, my dear! Of course not! I wouldn't have that life back for anything! No, not for anything!"

Ethel looked doubtfully at her mother, wondering how to take this *volte face*. Then, relaxing, she said softly: "To tell the truth, I don't know either. . . . Jack was a nice boy, and so kind. . . . He might have made me happy if I hadn't. . . ." She couldn't go on for the tears which had suddenly forced their way to her throat. With a desperate effort she hardened herself against them, and cried fiercely. "I'm talking tommyrot! . . . This is better, far better!" She laughed hysterically, alarming her mother, who, snatching at any straw, asked weakly:

"Can't you get interested in your art again? You haven't done a thing for ages!"

"Don't talk to me of art! What do I want with it? Other people may fool themselves by putting another daub in a frame, but what is that to me? What I want is life! Life! Life! . . . Don't you see, I am bored, bored. . . . Just as much bored, I dare say, as you were, when you pressed your face against the window and looked down that silly street. . . ."

"Many would envy you," rejoined her mother. "You're in Paris, the most wonderful city in the world. You . . ."

Just then a knock came, relieving the intolerable tension. Ethel opened the door and confronted the postman. He handed her a registered letter and asked her to sign.

When the postman was gone, Ethel remained standing for some moments contemplating the envelope, which bore a Polish stamp. The handwriting seemed so uncannily familiar yet so strangely remote. She knit her brows in perplexity.

"Whom is it from? Why don't you open it?" her mother urged her.

"Oh, I know!" Ethel exclaimed, her frown giving way to a faint eager smile. "It's from Jan!"

"Jan? What can he want?"

Yes, what could he want? It was six—or was it seven?
—years since Jan had so precipitately left her, having
given and taken away the first and last real happiness
she had known. And she had not heard from him since.
What object, then, could he have in writing at this late
date? With trembling hands she tore open the envelope.

There was a short note stating that he, Jan, would
within a week be leaving Warsaw for Paris and it would
give him much pleasure to renew their friendship. In a
postscript, he added—it seemed, with a cryptic chuckle
—that as members of her sex liked reading between
lines, she might read between his anything her heart
desired.

.   .   .   .

"That was a week ago," explained Mrs. Prescott, having given Mr. Rennell substantially the above account
of their lives. "And Jan's in Paris now," she added.
"Naturally, the poor child's disturbed. Of course, any
girl would at the prospect of again meeting the man who
first made her a woman, and a happy one!"

Rennell nodded sympathetically. But he was thinking
his own thoughts. He resented Jan's coming on the scene
at this juncture. As for the rest, it was much ado about
nothing.

"You must warn her she mustn't take up with that

Pole again," he said pontifically. "It never will do to recross old trails. I know. . . . I ought to know. . . ."

Yes, she thought, he, if any one, ought to know. He was no Puritan. . . .

"No. You mustn't let her meet Jan again," he repeated.

V

Ethel was accustomed to having her own way.

When she left her mother with Rennell, her own mind indeed was occupied with Jan. She was wondering if she ought to go see him right now. He had written her that he would be staying at the Hotel Regina on the Right Bank. He had arrived sometime that morning and sent her a "pneumatic" at once to tell her where he was. He would look out for her for dinner that night. That is, if she could come. He was aware of the notice being short and of the possibility of her not being able to come. In the latter event, he would look in at the flat sometime the next day. She had at first made up her mind that he should look her up. Her mother had concurred in the wisdom of this choice. It wouldn't do for Ethel to show her anxiety to see him. In any case, it was up to the man to make the overture. It was for the woman to run, for the man to pursue.

They no longer talked of the equality of men and women, of the freedom of women to do as they pleased. That was quite all right in theory. Men took such an advantage of a woman, once she put it into practice.

But because Jan was in town she felt nervous to the point of irritation. Rennell's appearance and his insistence on joining them intensified this mood. Besides, she saw her mother "making a fool of herself" over him, as she put it to herself. Her mother always seemed to lose her balance in the presence of celebrities, great and small. After all, they were but little different from other men. As for old Rennell, she thought him a fool. She did not want him around. Anyhow, not that evening. She had heard every one of his stories, and she didn't want him making eyes at her. He was positively maudlin the last time she had seen him alone. Made her a thousand promises if she'd only go off with him to some idyllic spot like the Balearic Isles or the Isle of Lemnos, wherever that might be. She now gave a fierce chuckle as the thought crossed her mind that if given time he might make the same proposition to her mother. From the bottom of her heart, she hoped he would. Let him try to paw over her mother as he had tried to paw over her. Just see how she'd take it. 'Twould serve her mother right for slob-

bering over a man like Rennell. She'd most likely begin
by telling him the story of her life, and all about her,
Ethel. Of course, she meant well. But that was her
mother. Well, what was to be done about it? She had
long since given up fretting. If only she could do something to banish her boredom! If only she could get interested in somebody or something!

She glanced at her watch. It was only half-past seven.
There was still time to catch Jan. He said he'd wait until
eight for her. Without further hesitation, she got into a
taxi and asked to be driven to the Hotel Regina.

All her thoughts turned to Jan. Why shouldn't she go
to him? Jan was in Paris, and it seemed so natural to see
him. Her mind, unhappy and distraught, appeared to
remain where it was when she had last seen him. It
found it hard to bridge the years which had flowed dully
by since those rapturous weeks and months when she
loved Jan and Jan loved her. Why had he left her when
he did? Had he really ceased to love her? She simply
refused to believe this. She liked to think that it was
something else, that it was perhaps Jan's restless adven-
turous spirit asserting itself in favor of the larger adventure. She liked him for that. She was ready to forgive his
thoughtless defection. She could not but believe that he
still entertained for her that older tenderness of his, and
could not conceive of a state in which Jan did not entertain it. Good Jan! If he was his old dear self, she would

not complain. So unsentimental of late, even hard (as she thought herself), the memory of those early happy days resurrected itself, and her heart fluttered with anticipation.

"I am silly, downright silly," she thought to herself. "I'm afraid I've had a drop too much. It's gone to my head. I shouldn't drink on an empty stomach. . . . Jan probably won't look at me. Who knows, I mayn't like him? . . . That would be terrible . . . not to like Jan! We did have such good times together. . . ."

She closed her eyes and, falling back against the cushions of the taxi, gave herself up to the dream of life cherished and gone by. But these past six or seven years . . . the lovers she had known. . . . Heavens, she had cared for none of them! Then why did she have them? Well, because she had been on the everlasting lookout for romance, always hoping to find that ultimate haven from which she need no longer set out adventuring. Lovers had become a necessity with her. Perhaps, not really a necessity; merely a bad habit, but still a habit and hard to break! She did enjoy them at moments in a fashion. But between these intense moments they were a vexation and a bore. How often she had tried to break away from it all, she had even contemplated going into a convent. . . .

Thus time went on, and she waited . . . waited for some one or something to turn up, to shake her out of

herself. Yes, here she was in "gay Paree!"—and to all
intents and purposes, like her mother had been in Biddlebury, Connecticut, her face pressed against a hypothetical window (real as any other!) and, with half
closed eyes of dream, looking down a long street, without any turning! O God! What was wrong with her?
What was wrong with everything? . . . And here was Jan
back again. Was it for him she had waited all these bar-
ren years? Would he rescue her from her plight, would
he restore her? She thrilled to his name, and she hoped
and despaired by turns.

The taxi was now crossing the bridge, the multiple
lights of the Place de la Concorde and the Champs
Elysées hove into view. Paris on a spring night was
charming, and this spot in her sight the most charming
of all. The taximan, a tall gaunt figure, with flaxen hair
and sensitive face with nothing of the Gaul in feature,—
doubtless a Russian prince in disguise—Paris was full
of such—drove in a roundabout way, as if unfamiliar
with the alien streets; but she did not care. The long-
drawn-out moments of anticipation were thereby further
prolonged. There was mysterious joy in this—and bitter
agony.

At last the taxi drew up before Jan's hotel. She paid
the driver, and entering the hotel, asked for Monsieur
Petchorski. Presently word came that he would be down
within five minutes. Ethel seated herself in the lounge

and, watching the clock, counted the minutes. Even while she was preoccupied with this, at the same time anxiously observing every passer-by, a half familiar jocular voice brought her back to herself:

"Well, well, if it isn't little Ethel!"

With startled eyes she looked at the man who addressed her and like one in a dream or trance tried to recall who she was, where she was, and why she was here. No, she mustn't drink again—not on an empty stomach. But here was a man talking to her, calling her by name, a shortish, plumpish man, with a huge gold watch-chain across his embonpoint and big rings on the stubby fingers of a pudgy hand stretched out to her in greeting.

"Ethel, don't you know me?" he asked, catching the look of incredulity in her eyes. "I am Jan, Jan Petchorski, at your service. I've changed, of course! People do change, you know. I'm fatter than I used to be. But you aren't changed a bit, Ethel, not a bit!" And he gave her an appraising glance, his eyes following from the fine curve of her neck and breast clear down to her slender ankles, mentally undressing her. "How do you manage it, Ethel? You're just right! 'Pon my word, just right!" There was eager anticipatory rapture in his voice.

"Please don't! Don't!" cried Ethel, like one stabbed and suffering agony. This lasted for some moments. Then, recovering from her panic, she laughed, rather boisterously for her, and boldly stretched out her hand. "Hello, Jan!"

The hurt look which had come into his complacent eyes disappeared. "That's better! That's better!" he said. "For a while I thought you were sorry to see me."

"No! No!" she hastened to reassure him. "I don't know what was the matter with me. But I have had a drink, and I'm afraid it went to my head!"

"I was hoping that I had!" he rejoined, laughing.

"There's no harm in hoping!" she replied enigmatically, by now in control of herself.

"That being the case, let's go out to dinner."

He took her to Weber's, in rue Royale, where, in the old days, they used to go sometimes, on gala occasions, when they were in funds.

He guided her to a little table in a corner which they used to occupy. She had wondered if he would remember. Then, glancing at the menu, he chose the items which used to be her favorites: *petite marmite,* grilled sole, duckling, asparagus, fresh raspberries and cream; and for wine Chambertin of a good vintage. Some of her confidence returned. He remembered everything. But how, in heaven's name, had he managed to get so fat? Why did he wear that awful gold watch-chain across his rather globular "tummy"? Why those heavy rings on the pudgy fingers? Why was his once unruly curly hair pomaded smooth and parted? Why was he altogether so different, with scarcely a vestige of his former self left?

He had developed some strange habits too since she had last seen him. He drew in his soup in a manner reminiscent of a suction-pump. While eating the fish, open-mouthed he leaned forward more than halfway to meet the over-laden fork. And, what she detested most of all, he tucked his table napkin into his waistcoat! What kind of associates had this man had in these past years to have produced such devastating effects on a once beloved mortal? The wine, 1891 vintage, helped to drown her embarrassment, her disappointment. She was even mildly amused at this fantastically absurd outcome to her expectations. And her very disappointment, deep as it really was, acted like a salutary shock, stirring her out of herself. If she had ever thought she had degenerated, sliding unhindered straight down hill, here was one, a darling of the gods she had thought him once, who already seemed at the bottom . . . a more self-satisfied, complacent soul she never hoped to see. Where, oh, where, was the fiery spark in his eyes which used to set her heart aflame? The wine flushed his face and enlivened his eyes, and the spark she looked for seemed several times on the verge of being born, but even while on the brink of birth it appeared to hesitate and withdrew, losing itself in the dark limpid depths whence it had come.

They had been exchanging trivialities when, after the fish course, Ethel abruptly asked:

"What are you doing, Jan?"

Jan gave vent to a mysterious knowing chuckle. "That can wait," he said. "Pleasure before business!"

"Business?" She opened her eyes wide, her thin long brows arched in curiosity.

He laughed again, and offered no explanation.

"Aren't you an artist any more?" she persisted in her inquiries.

"Certainly not! All that's nonsense. Art's all right in the wild oats stage of youth. But it won't do at all for a grown man! I've grown older and more sensible. . . . And are you going on with your art?" he pressed her with a smile.

"No," she reluctantly admitted.

"There!" he cried in triumph.

"I'm but a weak girl, with no talents," she asserted. "And art is not at fault. It's different with you. You're a man and you had the gift, and you should have gone on with what you started. You were beginning to be talked about too, were quite a celebrity in your way!"

"No, that's all nonsense! Not the work of a man. It pleased my fancy to put shoe buttons for eyes and glue discarded cigarette ends on canvas. If I had stuck it out, I should have gone in for Da-Da. And what was Da-Da? Nihilism, nothingness! Art's in a blind alley, and I was in a fair way of getting into one myself. No, all that's child's play! . . . The duckling's mighty good, I must say. . . . One has to live, you know!"

His blunt materialism awakened opposition in her. She felt deeply distressed by the change in him. And as she intently looked at him, searching as behind a mask for something of the man she had known and finding nothing there, she winced. How could she have loved this prosaic man? For she could hardly believe that any one could change so diabolically beyond recognition. Was she changing with the years herself? Had she also, relatively, changed as much as he for the worse? Had she a single illusion left out of the many with which she first landed on French shores? It appalled her, she felt frightened before the portentous shadows of approaching years. She was nothing, had nothing, not even a background. She was neither American nor French; neither an artist nor a bourgeois. She was a hanger-on, a parasite. And, oh, how dreadful it all was! As she looked round her, she saw happy faces; they were French. In the opposite corner an old couple attracted her. The man, about seventy, was hearty and hale, with ruddy cheeks above his white beard. The woman, slightly younger, had the grave contented face of one who has done her duty in this world. She was doubtless the mother of some sturdy sons and cheerful daughters. And she and the old man ate heartily and drank red wine, and laughed between mouthfuls. There was a quiet rustic air about them. She imagined they had come up from the provinces, and were perhaps celebrating their marriage day. A nostalgia seized Ethel for she knew not what. She wanted to hear different words from those to which she was being regaled by her host, hungered for other dishes than were to be found on that table. The duckling, she agreed, was good; the wine was excellent; but to-night they made a savorless meal.

She felt like crying. O God, wasn't there some one or something in this world that would renew her zest for life? No, no, it wasn't that. She had zest enough, it was life that was lacking. She was listening to a man who had once been alive and now was dead, and his words, which had at first deadened her feelings, now stirred her to revolt. She wanted to say, "You lie! You lie!" The wine she drank intensified this desire arising from the vision she saw of Jan as a gargoylish caricature of her former lover. Then, suddenly, she started from her perturbing reverie, as the word "Love" struck upon her ears. There, at last! What had he to say of love, this scarecrow who had once been a man? She bent forward to listen, not wishing to miss a word; for the restaurant orchestra had simultaneously struck up a loud piece. This was as good as opera.

"Love . . . of course, there's love. One can't do without love," he amended his previous statement, a lewd look creeping into his now ogling eyes. "Love makes the world go round. . . ."

"An original statement!" Ethel mocked him. "I thought it was wine. . . ."

"Love is a wine. . . ."

"That doesn't improve with years. . . ." Her malice was growing, she enjoyed mocking him.

"No, and that's a fact!" he rejoined. "A man naturally likes 'em young. He doesn't want duck when he's asked for duckling!" And Jan laughed almost a guffaw at his own jest.

"Which am I?" asked Ethel, out of curiosity, not without disgust.

"You?" he said, as lingeringly his eyes once more appraised her charms. "I think one may safely put you with the ducklings." And he struck up an attitude apparently intended to be gallant.

"Thank you. It took you rather a long time to arrive at a judgment. Well, you won't find me on the menu!" She felt ashamed and chagrined that she should have ever belonged to this man, and she wished she could find a way to hurt his feelings. Had he provided himself with a skin thick enough to resist her assaults?

"Well, I never!" he ejaculated simply, taking his rebuff good-naturedly.

It seemed to her that far from feeling hurt he was laughing at her. She, remembering their former intimacy, winced. The humiliation was almost more than she could bear.

"I don't know why you wanted to see me," she said, after a further exchange of equally inane flippancies.

"Why not? We are old friends. In any case, pleasure before business!"

"You've said that before," she retorted sharply, scarcely able to contain her irritation. "Why not now?"

"With coffee and liqueur, my dear. That's the practice, I believe, with all good Anglo-Saxons. Nothing like discussing business after a good lunch or dinner. It makes one feel so amiable!"

Was he being sarcastic? She could not tell from his manner. Serious or sarcastic, it seemed like an affront to her. She would have risen and flung out of doors, but her curiosity held her. What more had this uncouth man to say of interest to her?

With coffee and liqueurs before them, he was faithful to his promise.

"You're not particularly well off, are you?" he began. "I think you told me so."

"No. Mother lost some money lately in stocks. And we were not any too well off before."

"Exactly. I thought that might be the situation when I wrote you." He rubbed his hands, as if this intelligence was pleasing to him rather than otherwise.

What was he driving at? She looked mystified.

"It was a mere guess," he explained, catching her glance. "Most people with small incomes suffer sooner or later nowadays. . . ."

"Well. . . ."

"It occurred to me we might be of help to one another. I'm in the caviare business, and I need a representative for France and England. And I knew you spoke both languages. I would be willing to pay a handsome commission. . . . I . . ." And he went on and on to explain the nature of his business.

Dazed, she listened, without hearing, catching an isolated word here and there, as one catches words, with effort, from a wretched gramophone record.

It was buz-buz-buz—then the word "caviare"—then buz-buz-buz—then the word "per cent"—buz-buz—"earnings"—buz-buz-buz—"income"—buz-buz-buz-buz—"It's a fair offer"—buz-buz—"You can't do any better"—buz—"caviare"—"I thought of you"—buz-buz-buz—"best caviare in the market"—buz-buz-buz-buz-buz—"Think it over"—buz—"Caviare"—buz-buz-buz-buz-buz-buz-buz-buz-buz-buz-buz—

Thus, interminably, he went on, his smooth voice buzzing in her ear, which caught a stray word now and then, meaningless yet full of mysterious import. Then, all of a sudden, the sound of his voice ceased. She saw him draw a cigar from his pocket, watched him light it, then lean back in his chair comfortably. He seemed to wait, she watched him like one charmed. Why was he waiting? Moments passed, interminable moments, like abysmal vacuums opening vast maws to engulf her.... Words which had been spoken that evening came back to her out of the unconscious, like sleeping birds rooted out of their nests. . . . Da-Da!—nothingness—caviare—A vision of her mother talking animatedly with Rennell, as she had left them, rose before her. . . . He was saying something funny about the Pointillists—oh, yes, they had their points—that was it! And what did he say about the Sur-realistes? What—there, she remembered. They were so-real—so-real—no, no, it was different—she tried to think, to remember—oh, yes!—they were so-realistic —that was it—it was rather good too!—Two shoe-buttons for eyes—that was what Jan had said. She was getting mixed up—the wine must have gone to her head, she thought. She was watching Jan. He seemed to wait. Why was he waiting? Why didn't he speak? At last, to her relief, she saw his lips move, heard him speak.

"Well, my dear, what do you say to my caviare proposition?"

The words acted like a cold shower, awaking her. She leaned forward, and whispered, "Offer it to the general, my dear . . . or to the colonel . . . or . . ." She suddenly gave way to an outburst of hysterical laughter. She laughed loud and long, unrestrainedly, causing heads to turn to look at her; and tears ran down her cheeks from this excessive laughter.

"Don't! Please don't!" murmured Jan, alarmed by this exhibition of hysteria. "People are looking, Ethel! Every one's looking. Please don't!"

She paused as suddenly as she began. Her face was pale with anger, and her expression was one of utter and unutterable contempt. "So people are looking! That's what you're thinking of! Let them look! Let them! ... You think I'm hysterical. ... Well, I'm not! How should a girl act when a man who's been her lover makes her an offer to sell caviare? ... It's so funny, so funny!" And again she gave way to irrepressible laughter. Once more she paused, quite suddenly, as before. "I must go home!" she said soberly, rising from her chair.

"Wait a moment till I pay my bill. Then I'll take you home!"

"I want to go home alone," she said firmly, allowing of no doubt that she meant to do so.

He rose with her, beckoning to the waiter.

"Please don't!" she said, with a restraining gesture. "I shall be hysterical in earnest if you do! I'm better off alone!"

"I am sorry," he said, and made no effort to follow her, lest she carry out her threat.

Without another word, she left him.

She walked impetuously, followed by many curious

eyes. With unwonted vigor she pushed past the revolving door, colliding with a man about to enter and almost falling into his arms.

"Beg your pardon!" said the man in an American voice, softly, causing her to look up. The man recoiled, and looked at her intently. "Why, Ethel!" he cried. "Think of meeting you here!"

"Why, Jack! How did you come here? . . . It's wonderful to see you!"

Her words came from the heart, and he could not help detecting a note of distress in them.

"What's the matter, Ethel? Are you sick?" He asked in a voice at once tender and full of concern.

"Yes, Jack, I'm sick. Please take me home, Jack! You don't mind?"

"Me mind?"

And, without further word, he conducted her to a taxi. She gave directions to the driver and, like one in a dream, entered the taxi, which appeared as unreal as everything else that evening. Jack followed.

How strange everything was! She sank back against the cushions, ready to swoon from excitement, from the long gamut of emotions she had sustained, from the series of devastating moments, and of actions and reactions. She was in that hypnotic state when the tense moments of crisis are curiously a part of the blood, and, one by one, these moments, each an eternity, flow on with the

surging tide, suffusing the body with an unaccustomed
all-absorbing, all-enveloping fluid warmth. There was
a quickening of the senses, a bodily and mental exhila-
ration, attended by an outward quiescence as under the
influence of an opiate. Stirred to the depths as she had
never been before, she was yet held motionless, while
pleasing images flitted before her, and fancy upon fancy
swooped down, circling, and in snatches of persuasive
song bade her sit still. How long this spell of loveliness
lasted she could not later remember, but it was broken
by her own voice, and she listened to her voice as if it
were another's, while a hand—was it hers?—groped
for Jack's.

"Is it you, Jack? Really you?"

Ignorant of the mood which had given rise to her
strangeness, and not a little glad by her obvious delight
in seeing him, he matter-of-factly laughed, and said:

"Of course, it's I! Who should I be if not Jack?"

"You're not joking? Is it really you, Jack? Really
you?" She pressed his hand for confirmation.

"Yes . . . yes. . . . Can't you see?" He was beginning
to be concerned about her. She appeared to be talking
deliriously, as in a fever. If she was ill, why was she out
alone at night, and in Paris of all places?

As if she had scented the nature of his thoughts, she
said quietly:

"I'm not mad, Jack! Don't think me mad! But I've

suffered so many shocks to-night. I—you see— Oh, life's terrible, Jack! Terrible!"

"Don't talk about it to-night," said Jack reassuringly, conscious that it pained her to talk.

"And on top of it all, I had a glass or two of wine. Brandy too. It's gone to my head to-night. It doesn't usually. I don't know what's the matter with me to-night!"

"Never mind, Ethel! Don't think about it! Don't think about anything! What you need is bed and rest!" His voice was tender, there was a world of kindness in it. He patted her gently on the back. "There's a good child!" he went on, as under his ministrations she grew quiet, and her small warm hand lay quiescent in his.

Suddenly, without warning of any kind, a sob, a deep sob, broke from her. Then another. And another. Something in his voice had touched something in her hitherto inviolate. And that something in her, hard like a knot in the wood, melted like snow before a spring thaw, releasing gentle rivulets of tears. The tears gushed from her eyes, and in this gushing of tears was sweet agony and release from secret grief.

"There! There!" he went on patting her back gently. And her sobs ceased, she now wept quietly. This paroxysm had not lasted long.

She felt ashamed of herself and of her tears. "I'm sorry," she said. "I didn't mean to be a cry-baby!"

By now they had reached the street in which she lived. He got out and gave a hand to her.

She was more calm. "Jack," she said, "you'd better keep the taxi. I won't ask you in. Not to-night. Drop in to-morrow if you like. I'll be in all the afternoon. Apartment Six. Don't forget!"

He did not insist. She'd be better off alone the way she felt. "Very well, my dear!" he said, and, bending over, pressed his lips to her hand.

She withdrew her hand quickly and, with a rapid stride entering the open archway, vanished from sight.

After giving directions to the driver, he gravely and thoughtfully rcëntered the taxi.

VI

The next day, about three o'clock in the afternoon, he made his appearance. His broad erect six-foot frame almost filled the doorway, as he put a generous hand forward to shake Ethel's, while the premature furrows of his broad swarthy face mellowed into a series of curves to form a good-natured smile.

"Glad to see you," he said simply.

"The same here!" she heartily responded to his mood.

He seated himself in the large chair she offered him and, for some time, gazed in silence at Ethel, who seated herself in the chair opposite. Joyously his eyes fell on the silver bracelet she wore. He recognized it as the first thing he had given her in their courting days.

"Paris is fine," he said at last, to break the tension, "and the weather is fine, and I feel fine!" He spoke in a dry nasal twang, but it sounded pleasant because his voice was friendly and conveyed cheer.

"Yes, it's a lovely city," she agreed, "and spring is particularly lovely in Paris!"

"So I've heard. And I must say I'm not disappointed. Everything's in bloom, but where I come from April's pretty bleak. . . . Doesn't anybody ever work here? On a day like this, everybody seems to be out-of-doors, the cafés are full, and everywhere there's the look of a holiday!"

"When did you come?"

"A day or two ago."

"How long do you intend to stay?"

"I don't know. It all depends."

"You sound mysterious." She laughed.

"Not at all. I'm rather foot-loose just now. I expect to stay in Paris till I get tired of it. Then I shall follow where fancy leads!"

"You're getting more and more mysterious, Jack. What brings you here? Is that a secret?"

"You'll laugh if I tell you," he said, smiling with an embarrassed air, as if he were on the verge of divulging something of which he was ashamed.

"Don't tell me if you don't want to!" Half in earnest, she laughed.

"I guess this secret can stand the light of day," he replied with a twinkle in his eyes. "Anyhow, I hope so. . . . Well, it's this way. I've worked hard and I've made a heap of money. Yes, a great heap of money. Luck's had a hand in it, of course! And one day I got to thinking. Said to myself: 'Well, Jack old boy, what are you going to do about it? Here you are a good thirty years old, and you've enough money to keep you comfortable for the rest of your natural life. What are you getting for your money? You're living, and don't know why! What's it all about, anyway? Are you going to collect more and more money? Become a Ford, or a Rockefeller? As for that, what's Ford or Rockefeller getting out of it? Yes, Jack, you've got money to burn, and if the preachers are right about the camel and the eye of a needle, then by gad you'll go to the place where the greenbacks and the yellowbacks you've collected will only be used to sizzle your sinner's hide—and it's a fact! That won't do at all, Jack! The time has come for you to find out what it's all about, this game called life. . . .' I began to ask myself all sorts of questions. I kept awake nights, thinking and thinking: What's it all about? It became a sort of obsession with me. And yet no answer could I find. None at all. I knew there were other men in the same boat as myself, and I wondered if they asked themselves the same question, if any of them kept awake nights wondering what it was all about!

"The time came," Jack went on, with some fervor, "when I couldn't keep it to myself any longer, and I put the question straight to my partner. 'Well, Harry,' I put it to him, 'what's it all about? Why do you work like a slave? You have a fortune which will do for you until doomsday! Why are we hustling all the time, going round and round like squirrels in a cage, to all intents and purposes getting nowhere? In short, what do you and I get out of it?' Well, Harry gave me a queer look, I guess, to see if I looked like a candidate for Middletown —that's the place, you know, where we keep our lunatics in Connecticut—and seeing I was sober and in my right mind, he laughed and said: 'I've heard it said, Jack, that a fool can ask more questions than a wise man can ever answer!' Then I put the same question to other folk, and the stock answer was: 'Ask me another!'

"Well, pretty nearly everybody was dodging the issue, hiding their head like an ostrich, though now and then I found some one troubled like myself. One day I ran into an artist chap at Westport—that's the artist colony! —he was a man who lived in a bungalow studio, did most of his work, and seemed fairly happy. Said he to me: 'The secret of happiness is to love your work and mind your own business!' That set me thinking more than ever. Then there were others—a good many in fact— who said: 'Over there, in Europe, they know how to live. You won't hear a Frenchman asking your question!' I heard it so often that I made up my mind to come over and see for myself. I thought I ought to give myself a year, if I was to learn anything. So I left my partner in charge, and here I am, on a voyage of personal investigation. . . ."

He paused, and looked inquiringly at Ethel, as if anticipating an expression of her views.

"You can't do much in a year," she said. "It takes a year just to get used to things. There's old Wilfred Rennell. He said to mother only last night: 'Europe is nuance!' Yes, Europe is just that, and it takes a long while to be able to see the fine shades of things. . . ."

"Oh, do you know Rennell—the great Rennell?" Jack exclaimed.

"Yes. Why?"

"Why, because he writes great stuff! There's no one over there who can write like that. I got his last book, and I sat up well into the night reading it. It must be great knowing such people!"

Ethel smiled whimsically. It was just as she had felt about great men before she had come to Europe. "You are lovely!" she exclaimed. "Would you like to meet Mr. Rennell?"

"Wouldn't I just?" came the ardent response. "Could you manage it, you think?"

"Manage it? Why, Rennell would be delighted to meet you, I'm sure," Ethel replied ambiguously. "He likes Americans. Eats 'em alive, as you'd say!"

"Does he, really?" said Jack, suddenly grown timorous. "But what could I say to him if I met him?"

"Just tell him how much you like his books! You can't pile it on too thick! And just watch him lap it up. He'll appreciate you for being able to appreciate him. He's a good fellow in his way."

"That doesn't sound as if he were any different from the fellows I know in business," laughed Jack.

"No. Still, he does things of that kind like an artist!"

"Thank you so much, Ethel! . . . I must learn about this place Europe, and I scarcely know where to begin."

" 'Anywhere is a beginning!' So says a friend of mine who's given up the pork business in America to write poetry."

"That's pretty good," he agreed. "Then I'll begin right here, if you don't mind. You've already taught me a lot as it is!"

"Of course!" Ethel was amused. "I think I'll start an Institution for the Education of Innocents Abroad!"

"A jolly good idea! You might take me on as your first pupil."

"It's a bargain," she said.

"Shake on it!" And he extended an earnest hand.

There was a silence. Then Ethel, quite abruptly, asked:

"I wonder what you thought of me last night."

"It was perfectly marvelous to run into you!" he said, after slight hesitation.

"You're a dear to say that. But you are dodging my question!"

"Am I?" he appeared embarrassed, and his eyes were directed on the rug. Then he braced himself, looked squarely into her eyes, grown wistful with troubling thoughts which he wished he could fathom and assuage. "You see, my dear," he said gently, "I know hardly what to say. I don't know what happened last night. I saw you were in trouble, and I wanted to help you. That was all. . . . And yet, of course, I want to be honest with you," he went on, after a pause. "I'm only human, I suppose. I was curious—not that I'm trying to make you say anything now—I only say this because you asked, and because you expect me to be frank. Yes, I was curious. But I didn't think ill of you—not at all—it's not for me to judge—I don't want to judge! I guess that artist chap was right—one of the secrets of happiness is to mind one's own business. Please don't think anything more about it!"

"But I *want* you to know," she said, faintly smiling—it was the same wistful smile that first awakened his intimate interest in her. "I hate mysteries and secrets. And I don't want you to think me either better or worse than I am. You admitted you were curious. . . ." She saw pain cross his features and a visible effort to repress some inner struggle. Her voice faltered, as she went on: "I was dreadfully upset last night. You see, I went to dinner with a man who once meant something special to me, and I found him so utterly, utterly impossible.... He had been an artist.... I expected to meet an artist...." She smiled ruefully. "I found a keen business man, who wanted to see me because I might be useful to him. He wanted to give me a job...." Her voice broke, perturbed by the humiliating memory.

"Please don't!" said Jack gently. "I quite understand! I quite understand!" He didn't understand at all, but he felt dreadfully sorry for her, and he wanted to take the pain from her.

"Forgive me," she said. "I forgot you were a business man. You somehow don't seem like one. At any rate, you're a gentleman...."

"Thank you," he said, laughing.

"I did want you to know why I blubbered last night. It was such a shock to me.... And then ... You turned up. You don't know what it meant to me at the time. You were so kind, so considerate.... I'd almost forgotten such people existed.... You were all the more nice because I must have looked dreadful. You know I did. I know I felt dreadful. . . ." She was thinking in particular of her rouged lips.

The impulse she had had to tell him everything, without reserve, gradually vanished in the friendly atmosphere created by her attractive visitor. She had to confess to herself that he had some curious charm and that in her sober mood of the afternoon she liked him as well as in the distraught moments of last evening. She could not analyze the nature of her liking. Not bad-looking, he could scarcely be called handsome. But there was something fine and honest and sterling about him; "clean," she had unconsciously said to herself, with no intention of using the word as the opprobrious epithet that it was in circles in which she associated. She could hardly explain it, but it was as if a refreshing coolness emanated from him; the coolness of a sylvan spring, never more welcome than when the thirst of the weary traveler has reached the unbearable intensity of a long abstaining. In her case, it was "cool water after cocktails," as she put it to herself, and she flattered herself on the apt image. She could not, and would not—not at this juncture—tell him the whole truth. It was like slinging mud into the clean pool, she had neither the heart nor the mind to soil it, even just as she was slaking her thirst.

She felt that, perhaps, she ought to run; and yet she was half afraid lest he should run. It was an uncomfortable position for her who, for all her sins, had never resorted to deliberate dishonesty. She merely said:

"You may not know it, but you saved my sanity last night."

"I am glad," he said simply, while a pink flush suffused his face.

The novelty of seeing a grown man blush gave Ethel, used to hardened males, a curious unaccustomed pleasure.

No, decidedly she could not spoil the afternoon and their renewed friendship by gratuitous self-exposure. She derived some little satisfaction from the fact that she had tried to tell him and received discouragement. Her feminine curiosity, too, perhaps unconsciously, deterred her. There were aspects here which made her speculate and wonder. Life was amusing again. For the first time in heavens knew how long she could show an interest in the future. Her life had suddenly gained a new direction, a new zest. With the unfailing intuition which women often have she detected tokens of the old flame which slumbered and, given sufficient provocation, was ready again to burst forth. She wanted to be honest and fair with him. Well, there would be plenty of time to act accordingly, should the occasion arise. There was no real need of precipitating matters. Everything in life had its own appointed hour. She must wait for its summons and obey it when it came. Only puritans, she thought, carried that eternal burden of conscience which hindered their taking flight into the very care-free regions of supra-moral fancy. Thank heaven, she had rid herself of the superfluous ballast ages ago! One by one, she had thrown overboard her stock of inhibitions, and she took lightly certain matters, the very thought of which would have made her grandmother squirm.

She had once loved this man, he had been her first love. Several romantically-intended but too earthly loves had obscured but not crushed the memory of his having been the first to awaken her tender mood, in its more delicate moments resembling the trembling of a leaf, now too rarely encountered. Those remembered moments had suddenly become precious, and she experienced the most unaccountable yet very real desire, not to be repressed, of seeing their resurrection. She could not understand it: in the presence of this man she felt virginal again. It was a strange and fascinating experience. And she had thought herself too jaded ever again to give way to such innocent, foolish fancies. Yet there was a significant difference: she could not deny being conscious of the intervening years, which now erected themselves, as it were, into a wall between her and this man, a wall not easily surmounted. This circumstance added piquancy to the situation, gave birth to acute expectancy. If love was the all-powerful thing the romantics gave it the credit of being, then before its sonorous blast the wall of these years should crumble like the wall of Jericho before the blast of the trumpets of Israel.

Where did these thoughts spring from? Why did they agitate her so, endowing her with a strange new hope when she thought all hope was lost? As yet nothing tangible had happened, and there was little to justify her mood. With feminine prescience, she awaited the revelation, and like a flower closing its petals at twilight rested expectant of the dawn, which would bring the new unfolding.

VII

They went to cafés, restaurants and museums together. She showed him the Paris she knew. It included many a haunt unknown to the casual tourist.

One unostentatious little café in the Place Pigale, in Montmartre, particularly fascinated him; and in a remote way it touched upon his own inner problem. Here, in a modest back room, whose walls were lined with the usual plush-backed seats, you drank your beer or sipped your *fin*, while in the center, upon a dais, obscure native bards, with not a little gusto, recited aloud their poems. Jack was astonished to learn that one fine fellow with dark curly hair and a spark in his brown eyes, who read his poetry with especial vim, was a poet only by night, and a clothes presser by day; that another, a dapper little man with graying hair, no longer young, was a government clerk; that a third, a man of about forty-five, the father of seven children, was an adept in the application of the old-fashioned remedy of cupping and massage—no vestige of middle age was manifest but an abundance of undying spirit uncrushed by the material exigencies of time. There were others here, each taking his turn on the small platform with zest, in order to make known to a small world his heart's dream. Unknown and unsung, these men appeared marvelously alive and enjoying a measure of happiness; and whether their poetry was good or bad Jack did not know and did not care. What was important was that their voices vibrated with excitement, with life; and there were moments of visible ecstasy in their eyes and on their lips. Their ardent temperament, expressed in an unknown tongue, communicated itself to him, filling him with a curious delight and with feelings hitherto remote and strange. And it made him feel tenderly towards the girl at his side. He turned to her and said:

"Here, in this place, I've come nearest to having my question answered."

"What question?"

"The question I've been asking myself and everybody, 'What's it all about?' "

"Oh that! I should have thought, Jack, that you'd be asking your question more than ever here!"

"In your way you're right," he said. "But what I

mean is that these men make me feel that asking questions is foolish, and that if one only lived ardently and intensely one might forget to seek ultimate justification for existence!"

"You're an apt pupil, Jack," she commended him. "You've improved wonderfully since I took charge of your education six weeks ago. Only don't go on improving out of recognition. I like you as you are!"

Thus encouraged, he smiled tenderly on her. As yet he had not spoken of his innermost feelings towards her, which were growing apace. Perhaps, there was no need to speak. His every glance and every petty act assumed the guise of tacit grace towards her person.

He asked her earnestly about every manner of subject. Sitting at the Dome one evening and surveying the crowded tables spread along the pavements, he said:

"I'm told there are forty thousand painters in Paris. What becomes of them all?"

"I can answer for one," she answered, laughing. "Look at me, one of the forty thousand! See for yourself! I'm a typical case. What's become of my art?"

"Yes, what's become of it?" he urged her to an answer. "You had considerable talents, if I remember right!"

"No, no, Jack! I'm a good-for-nothing! And there are a good many like me here—all good-for-nothings!"

"Why did they go in for art?" demanded Jack, puzzled.

"That's easy to answer. They hated business—the humdrum existence! They took up with art as a sort of escape, just as I've done. Not that it is an escape. . . ."

"Ah, I see. . . ." And Jack became thoughtful. Since coming to Paris, infected by the atmosphere into which he had been plunged, he had seriously thought of beginning painting lessons himself. It would give him something to do; for he had not acquired the art of idling gracefully, and there was little likelihood that he would. Her answer gave him food for thought. "What a terrible waste!" he murmured at last.

"Americans always think in terms of utility, of economics," she chided him.

"And why not?" he retorted. "It's a tragic thing to see so many souls wasted!"

"What would you have them do?"

"Buckle down to work!"

"No one would want their product. There are too many of them. They'd run up against the law of supply and demand, or whatever you call it. Your economics work both ways!"

"What a pity!" he said. "I have you particularly in mind, Ethel. Promise me, you'll resume your art work to-morrow. I'll appoint myself your patron and buy every daub you paint!"

"You don't understand," she returned. "It isn't altogether the money. It's that I'm no longer interested in art!"

"It's good to be occupied. Necessary, I should say. . . . Do it for me!" he pleaded. The last word escaped him involuntarily. It was the nearest he had come to a declaration.

She looked at his earnest face, all screwed up into a plea, and she smiled a friendly, resigned smile.

"Very well, Jack. I'll do it for you. Only don't blame me if it doesn't pan out as you expect. Only I must have a proper studio with north light. And I must have models when I want them! I can't afford it, really. And I can't let you pay!"

"Nonsense!" he overruled her. "Let me attend to all that. All I ask is a part of your product, and we'll call it square!"

He persuaded her. Once persuaded, she welcomed the idea. She had always wanted a studio, a place to which she could retire without being within the immediate call of her mother. She wanted it for her mother's sake as well as her own. They were at times the source of great vexation to one another. She was dreadfully sorry for her mother, and she had reasons to know that her mother was dreadfully sorry for her. After all, whatever her mother's faults, she had given her daughter everything. It had been a mistake, of course, but she meant it all for the best. Ethel felt that she had failed her mother, and the sense of her failure deeply troubled her. It was hard on them both.

Jack, secretly, also liked the idea of Ethel having quarters away from her mother. He didn't think her mother was a good influence. Besides, he had known all the time that Mrs. Prescott had been responsible for Ethel's departure for Europe and the breaking of their engagement; he mistrusted her. It was true, Mrs. Prescott had at the beginning shown a decided predisposition towards him, and he at one time suspected that nothing would have pleased her more than to see them united in the holy bonds of matrimony.

Such indeed was the case. Mrs. Prescott warmly welcomed the advent of Ethel's first admirer. She saw it break the long stretch of unhappiness. It had given them both a breathing-spell from that wretched condition commonly called "getting on each other's nerves." Then a new factor entered, that parodoxical irony inherent in certain human natures which cannot leave well enough alone. For as Ethel grew happier and her intimacy with Jack developed, her mother not only felt "left out" but found herself resenting the influence Jack exerted in drawing Ethel away from the life she had so ardently desired to give her. And as she found her own power on the wane, she both consciously and unconsciously began to throw out insidious hints about Jack's intellectual deficiencies, his puritanic inhibitions bound to make any modern young woman unhappy, his obtuseness and out-of-placeness in the company of artists, and about his peculiarly American sentimentality which was sure to make him a laughing-stock among the purlieus of the City of Light. Even his perhaps foolish generosity in over-tipping the waiters, a practice commonly frowned upon in the Latin Quarter, was counted against him. Jack really hadn't a leg to stand on, though Mrs. Prescott's method of amputation had nothing of bluntness; she employed the most delicate knife and most skilled anæsthetics, leaving wounds and pain of which one was conscious only afterwards. Apart from this, she casually, with increasing frequency, dwelt on her own former life in Biddlebury, Connecticut; on the deadliness of lovely antiques, and on the dreariness of having to stand, hour after hour and day after day, looking out of the window, in the expectation of something happening which never did happen. On an impressionable girl like Ethel, the effects produced were little short of devastating. An atmosphere was created in which the subtle hostilities of the protagonists played upon one another; and between Jack and her mother Ethel's life had become a seesaw of unceasing uncomfortable balancings, and more of a problem than ever.

This tacit intangible factor had something to do with Jack's proposal to furnish Ethel with a studio, and mutely, in their heart of hearts, both Ethel and Jack jumped at the idea with eager if repressed alacrity.

Two days later Jack arrived with beaming face to announce to Ethel that the thing had been accomplished and that a lovely studio, fully furnished, was awaiting her occupancy. She rewarded him with a grateful look, full of significance. Jack was radiantly happy.

VIII

Ethel was delighted with the studio. It was a very large, very high room, with small kitchen on the same floor, and with a narrow little stairway leading to the gallery, which harbored a bedroom. There were two divans piled with multi-colored cushions, a long antique oaken table, a davenport facing the fireplace, two or three comfortable chairs and equal number of straight-backed ones, all antiques; and at the back of the room was a dais for the model to sit or to stand. Jack had leased it for a year from a wealthy American woman, who was not an artist and who used it for dancing and entertainment, to which purposes, to the chagrin of artists, and to the tune of thousands of francs, not within the purse of would-be Titians and Michelangelos, most of the old Paris studios were now dedicated. There were vases of roses in profusion on the table, on the mantel-piece and on the long window sill.

Ethel gasped when she saw it all and observed the thoughtfulness that had gone into the preparation for her coming. Spontaneously she flung her arms around Jack's neck and gave him a smacking kiss.

"How wonderful! You're a dear! How did you manage to get the studio?" exclaimed Ethel, clapping her hands. "No one but an American millionaire can afford one of these now."

"You've answered your own question," said Jack, flushing with pleasure.

"It's almost too comfortable to work in!" she said. "I shall want to lie on a divan and munch bon-bons."

They decided on a house-warming, and they debated a long time as to whom to have and whom not to have. Jack objected to Rennell being asked.

"I don't like the man," he said.

Ethel smiled. "I thought he was one of the men you were dying to see!"

"So he was! I had the mistaken notion that a man who could create such a fine self-sacrificing hero as Samuel Daw must be a fine man himself."

Ethel gave vent to an amused snicker.

"I guess," went on Jack, in his dry Yankee fashion, "our friend, Mr. Rennell, gets all his sacrifice out of his system by putting it into his characters!"

"Over on this side," observed Ethel, "we judge a man by what he is, not by what he does. Rennell is a man of genius, and a man of genius may commit arson and rape, and is all the more thought of on that account!"

"Huh!" Jack gave an expressive grunt.

"You must forget your New England notions on this side," Ethel gently admonished him. "We simply can't afford not to ask Rennell."

Jack gave in. He hadn't liked the way Rennell ogled Ethel; he was also conscious of Rennell's hostility to him. "The man's a vulture," he asserted grimly.

The party was scheduled to take place in the evening. In the early hours of the afternoon Ethel, assisted by Jack, worked to prepare the place for the prospective visitors. When their work was finished they sat down to tea. After they had had their last cup, Jack, without warning, sprang the question:

"Ethel, will you marry me?"

Ethel did not reply at once. The color in her face came and went, and she sat in her chair still and mute, like one without volition or voice.

"What's the matter?" he cried, flinging himself at her feet and looking up into her so wistful face. "What's the matter?" he repeated. "I didn't mean to hurt you? Oh, what have I done?"

She languidly let her hands fall on his head, and she slowly ran her fingers through his hair, caressing him

gently yet with painful will-lessness, as it were automatically.

She braced herself, and began to speak in an unsteady
voice.

"Jack, I'm very fond of you, I think I love you. I
don't want to say No, yet I hesitate to say Yes. I think
you ought to know more about me before we take such
a serious step. On the first day you came to see me, I
tried to tell you, to hint to you about the sort of girl I
am. I'm not sure you understood me. And I truly hadn't
the heart to go into details. Perhaps I should have. . . .
I don't know. Anyhow, I didn't. I . . ."

"Please don't!" he interrupted with a cry. "What
does it matter? What does anything matter? I love you,
and you love me, and there's nothing else!"

"You ought to know the truth, Jack. I don't want you
to find it out later, from some one else. You are straight,
and you are honest, and you are clean. Yes, clean! I
don't want you to say or to think afterwards that I've
deceived you, have been less honest with you than you
with me!"

"I don't . . ."

"No, no! Please don't interrupt! Please hear me out!
I owe it to you. You've been very good to me. You're the
kindest man in the world. I can't tell you what it's meant
to me—your kindness, I mean. When I first met you here
in Paris, I was going to pieces. And you've put me to-

gether again! . . . I shall never forget it, Jack. . . . I shall always . . ."

"Tut! Tut! Don't speak of it!" he again interrupted her, in spite of her admonition. "I deserve no credit for that. If I've done anything, I've had the pleasure of doing it. And I've had to do it!"

"That's what I like about you," she returned softly. "You are one of those sterling, honest persons, rare at any time. And you deserve something better than me who is like a weather-cock blown by every wind!"

"You've been perfectly angelic!" he protested.

"For how long? . . . I mean, how long am I likely to remain angelic, as you call it?" She smiled through her slowly forming tears, and there was so much sadness, so much wistfulness in her smile that if he did not take his eyes away he felt that his heart would break. That look in her eyes drew all his chivalry. He stood ready to exonerate her, to take all her sin on his own shoulders. "Listen to me!" she said with sudden desperation. "I tell you I have no character. I am swayed this way or that, according to who's with me!"

"You ought to get away from here, Ethel! From everybody!" pleaded Jack. "Let me take you away! Let me . . ."

"No, no, Jack! I know you mean mother. No one knows mother's weakness better than I. She's, perhaps, more sinned against than sinning. You know what a strait-laced community she came from. Her mother and father didn't get on, and she had a husband who was kind but hadn't an ounce of imagination. He was forever making her comfortable, giving her things.... And all the while she was yearning for life, real life, which she's never had. Well, she's tried to save me from all that. She's tried to live through me by giving me everything she's wanted herself and has never had. So she's brought me over here and she's tried to give me art and a full life, and because she's failed her position is pitiable. I'm ever so sorry for her, and she has to bear my resentment against her! For I often think that perhaps if I had never known this life, things might have been different. Who knows? I might have been happy. ..." At this point her voice faltered, became tremulous. With an effort, she went on. "I might have been happy with you, Jack, if I had never come to Europe. Now, Jack, I'm poisoned with Europe! D'you understand what that means, Jack? I can never be happy anywhere. I'm poisoned with a kind of corruption. Oh, it's so hard to explain, my dear! It's as if the place were a pile reeking with maggots, and one were a maggot oneself...."

"Chuck it all! And run away with me, my dear heart!"

"That's the awful part of it, Jack! It's hard to get away. We're all maggots here, but anyhow, we're alive, alive! There's no life where I came from. My mother spent day after day, year after year, looking out of the window, waiting for something to happen, which never did happen.... One's just caught, Jack! Caught! Between the deadness of Biddlebury and the corrupt aliveness of Europe!"

"There must be some way out! There surely must be some place in this world where you and I can get away and lead a different kind of life!"

"I don't know, Jack. I often find myself loving it all. The other day I was walking along the Montparnasse thinking of Biddlebury; rather friendlily too, and longingly. Then I caught sight of all the little tables of the Rotonde in the sun, and I saw a little group of Russians I knew, and they were discussing some subject animatedly, as if their life depended on it. And I knew they were honest, and in their way happy, in spite of misfortune. All at once I realized that the fault lay not with the place, but with me, and I warmed to it all, to all these people sitting at the little tables enjoying their modest drink in idleness. And I knew I could never go back to Biddlebury. Never, Jack!"

"But I don't ask you to go back to Biddlebury, my dearest! We can stay over here somewhere. Or we can travel. When we get tired of that, we'll take a house in town or in the country, and settle down for a bit. And we might have a little garden full of lovely flowers, and maybe later a baby son or a baby daughter, or both. We could—"

Ethel suddenly broke down and wept. He took her in his arms and, kissing her, tasted of the salt of her tears. When some minutes later she recovered from her outburst she sprang from his knee and seated herself at his side.

"Listen to me, Jack," she said, in a voice fraught with resolution. "Before we come to a decision I want you to know what a wicked woman I am. Maybe you've already guessed. I don't know. I've had several lovers. . . ." As she uttered these words, she intently watched his face to observe their effect. He was prepared for the revelation, and he hardened his heart against it and did not flinch. "And this isn't the worst of it," she went on. "I truly loved only the first. Even he wasn't worth it. Only I didn't learn it till the night I met you. He was the man I had dinner with. . . . I am a romantic fool. . . . After Jan—that was the first—I imagined myself again in love. . . . I'm a fool, I tell you! I'm a trusting nature, and I was deceived. Then I reacted against myself. I thought I was too soft. I went in for experiments. Love— if you can call it that—became a pastime! Are you horrified?" She laughed nervously, and again looked at him narrowly to see how he was taking it.

"How could you, Ethel?" His voice was censorious, yet full of pity.

"There, you wince!" cried Ethel. "Well, if you'd like to know, it's because I felt troubled, and intolerably bored. And because I think I must be naturally a wicked woman!"

"No, no, you're not!" he protested, but his voice was tired; it had lost some of its heartiness, some of its assurance. Propping his head on his elbows, he lapsed into troubled thought. It was clear that a struggle was going on within his heart and mind.

"Poor Jack!" she murmured, running her fingers softly through his hair. This had a strange soothing, almost hypnotic effect on him, and he resisted the more powerful impulse to seize her in his arms and wreak upon her a perversely awakened passion whose presence he had scarcely hitherto suspected.

She, for her part, was foundering in a not dissimilar welter of emotion. With a prescience, potently feminine, she saw they were approaching a climax; spurred on by words and circumstance, the moment of action was nigh. Why did he hesitate? Why didn't he seize her in his arms and crush her to him? Why didn't he grow angry, explode, do something, say something? She was helpless now with self-laceration. She was like a long-besieged, long-hungering city, succumbing at last, waiting for the conqueror to come and take possession. She had confessed her sin, she had betrayed her weakness, she was a supplicant ready to pay tribute, to be despoiled!

His hesitation was palpable. On the surface he was calm, but within, in the deeps of him, was such a whirl-

pool of emotion as he had never experienced; it held
him still, rendered him incapable of stirring. She, noting
only his hesitation, was like one observing the still sur-
faces of the whirlpool, scarcely suspecting the wild tur-
bulence underneath. Why, oh why, did he hesitate? Had
she not prostrated herself before him, humiliated herself
in contrite acquiescence to his attitude to life? Her
breaking heart desperately cried: "I am yours, only if
you'll take me. Only if your love is great enough in a
single virile gesture to sweep away the past and the dead
memories of all the spurious conquerors who have laid
low my heart!" But her lips were mute. She was wondering: was he weighing if she were worth the taking? Was
he going to retreat just as she had hoisted the white flag
of surrender? It surely looked like it. If only the drums
of triumph should beat now! Instead, there was dead
silence.

At last, after long instants, eternities, she heard a
voice—was it his?—the words came slowly and softly,
sounding like faint murmurings, like the dribbling of
a gentle rain against the walls of her enveloping mood,
expectant of hammer blows, of drum beats of triumph.

"My dear, my dear! Let's forget the past. Let's you
and me begin life anew, as if the old life didn't exist.
Promise me, you won't think of it, that you'll live for
me as I for you, that ..."

Heavens! What was he saying? She heard words,

words, and they seemed to convey no comprehension to her, but trailed off among the twilight shadows of some remote world almost out of hearing and quite out of reach. And she had wanted drum beats!

"Dearest, dearest," the voice went on, droning gently in a kind of monotone, softly tapping, tapping on the outer shell of her outer self, "I love you. Your past is past. Be a good wife to me now, and all will be well. . . ."

But her inner self was attuned to drum beats!

He was wondering why his words brought no response. Yet he was not altogether astonished. He himself felt curiously as if it were not the deeps of him that spoke, but as if his words were the external effulgence of a hollow sphere which passed by his name. He thought: he must remain true to character, true to self. By kindness and goodness he had won her; by kindness and goodness he must hold her. He did not know that in the storms of human emotion the thunder of the spirit is heard but the soft voice overwhelmed. And so it was when he should have shouted a command, he contented himself with soft murmuring, so that he could scarcely hear his own voice.

"My dear heart," he went on, gently pleading. "I don't want to hurry you into doing something you're not sure of. I want you to come to me of your own free will. Please think it over if you think it best. I'll come for my answer to-morrow, or the day after, as you decide!"

By now she had come to herself. "Yes," she echoed his words, "you'd better think it over, and come to me to-morrow, or the day after. And you can tell me then if, after what I've told you, you still want me!"

"Of course I want you!" he cried assertively. "There's no question of that at all. But I love you too well to try to force your hand if you still have doubts! ... If you have none, my dear, marry me at once, this very day. . . ."

She laughed. "No, not to-day, Jack. Remember it's already five o'clock, and there's that party to-night!"

"That's so, hang it! To-morrow then. What do you say to to-morrow?"

"Come to-morrow, and I'll give you my answer," she said, without giving the definite promise he expected.

In any case, the moment for action had passed. And he knew it, and she knew it.

IX

At nine o'clock the guests began to arrive. The first to come were David Barfus and his wife. Barfus was a rather handsome dark Jew of about thirty, by vocation a poet. He had once held a lucrative position in his father's firm, a traveling job which consisted in convincing the meat-shop proprietors of the Middle West of the superiority of his father's products to those of any other concern in the same line. These consisted of pork, bacon and pork sausages. His father, though an Orthodox Jew, professing the faith of his fathers in every detail and most scrupulously eschewing pork and similar non-kosher foods from his diet, saw nothing inconsistent in selling the vile abomination to gentiles, and was commonly spoken of in the community in which he lived as the "pork king." The Lord of the Hosts, far from frowning upon him, blessed him with prosperity. The son, David, who had leanings towards the *intelligentzia* and an inordinate love of poetry, more and more began to wonder why he should be selling pork when the only desire he had in the world was to write poetry. Pork and poetry, somehow, didn't mix! So having saved up a small sum of money, he one day announced to his father that he was quitting and going with his wife and child to Paris. "How are you going to live?" inquired his father. "Other poets manage somehow to exist, and I suppose I shall!" Whereupon his father pronouncing him *meshugah*—mad—asserted that if he persisted in his absurd resolution, he would not get a penny of his money. "Very well," said the son, and next day engaged third-class tourist passage on the first outgoing liner. The little money he had saved up was long since gone, and he and his small family, helped now by his friends, now by the surreptitious efforts of his mother, managed to exist, though it was a very meager existence. Barfus, however, managed to be cheerful, and often gay, and was, in consequence, a popular member in the Quarter. Jack grew particularly fond of him, and found devious ways of slipping him an occasional twenty-dollar note, without the other ever knowing the source of the welcome benefaction. His wife, a charming little chatterer, augmented the family income by doing odd typing jobs for her husband's friends.

By the time the first comers had been regaled by the energetic Mrs. Prescott to cocktails and sandwiches, other guests arrived, mostly painters from the American colony, one or two quite casually bringing their mistresses, free native-born Americans like themselves. A few of them had lived in Paris for so long, without re-visiting their native land (a matter of economics!), as to be in some difficulty with their paternal government, which ostensibly wasn't there to make easier the lot of the *émigré* but to facilitate his or her return that they might share in the peculiar benefits afforded, such as Prohibition, the flivver, the country club and the hundred other activities which made life so thrilling. Among the guests was Samuel Moody, a good New Englander, who had shown such promise with a first book of verse that he was immediately dubbed the "white hope of poetry in America," which was enough to disconcert any sensitive man. He had come over six years before for a brief visit, but became so enamored of the easy continental life that he vowed he'd never return to his native land. And, certainly, it looked as if he would keep his word, for he was going through the process commonly called "drinking oneself to death," producing between drinks lyrics of singular beauty. But he was not long for this world. It was said of him that he spent his life reeling: he reeled from having his thirst satisfied, and he reeled from sheer hunger. He made his

choice, he knew what he wanted. He preferred drinking
to eating. There was something about him which, in
spite of his inebriate state, made him respected. Besides,
he was one of those who in his worst moments remained
a gentleman.

The last of the guests to arrive was Rennell, who
brought with him a handsome tall dark energetic Englishman whom he introduced as Rufus Middleton.

"Not *the* Middleton?" asked Mrs. Prescott, in a
hushed voice, all agog at the mention of the well-known
name.

"Yes, *the* Middleton, the best painter in England to-
day!" the young man spoke up for himself. Then, good-
naturedly mimicking the American accent, he added:
"Yes, I'm the main cheese, the only pebble on the beach,
as you'd say in your country. For testimonials, I turn to
my esteemed friend here, Mr. Rennell. I say, old Ren,
do put in a word for me—to the ladies, I mean—I am
for standing strong with the ladies, the sugar and salt of
the earth!" And he slapped the older man on the back.
"No, no!" he turned to Ethel, who stood lost in admiration of his good looks, robust health and ebullient spirits.
"I'm no little tin god on wheels, but the real thing, Miss
Prescott, the real thing! Put me to the test, and see. I
am really!"

Ethel, amused, replied: "Oh, I'm willing to take your
word for it!"

"Please don't!" he rejoined, drawing her aside, while his companion was exchanging greetings with the other guests. "It's so deucedly unsatisfactory to be taken for granted. It leaves one nothing to do!" He smiled upon her energetically. "I hear you paint!"

"A little," she replied, modestly, overawed by his attentions.

"Too bad!" he laughed enigmatically.

"Because I paint little, or because I paint at all?" she asked, with a mock appearance of injury.

"Why should I do tribute to your painting? Especially when the painter herself is—" He did not finish his sentence, but made a gesture which conveyed a compliment.

"Blarney!" cried Ethel, amused, and even more pleased.

The young man began to make an earnest protest when an interruption came from Rennell who, at the behest of the still perturbed and purring Mrs. Prescott, desired to introduce his "distinguished friend" to the rest of the company.

The evening proceeded, as such evenings do, in the usual fashion: in chatter, badinage, discussion of arts and letters, gossip, punctuated by imbibings of wine, cognac, cocktails, and black coffee, and the munching of sandwiches. Jack, while keeping in the background, had his eyes and ears open; he was still trying to find out what it was all about, which was the object of his grand tour. These people did not help him much, for while they were interested, each in his particular art or his individual material problem, scarcely one ever touched upon the one thing which, in his opinion, really mattered. Only they seemed more satisfied than he, more happy than he. He was confused, an inner distress possessed him, he felt less happy than he had been in days. Yet never had Ethel appeared more charming. She wore one of those new high-waisted, long-skirted filmy frocks, which set off her natural grace and lovely head. Her face was flushed, her eyes alight as with a secret flame; every one openly expressed his or her admiration. Again and again he saw Middleton hover round her. It was clear to every one that Ethel had made a conquest. Mrs. Prescott went on asking questions of Rennell about him. Some one announced that the sandwiches were exhausted, and Ethel rose from her place to prepare more. Middleton, who happened to be sitting near her, offered his assistance.

"Sit still!" she said. "It won't take me a jiffy!"

"But preparing sandwiches is my *forte* in life!" he insisted. "I just love preparing sandwiches!" And he followed laughing Ethel into the kitchen.

They worked fast, and the sandwiches were soon ready. Ethel took the plates in her hands and was about to carry them into the studio when Middleton seized her pretty head between his two hands and fiercely pressed his lips on hers. She gave a faint gasp, cried, "Please don't!"—but warmed by drink and electrified by the passionate contact made no real resistance. He whispered something in her ear, and let her go.

Jack alone had observed their absence, and felt uncomfortable. He suddenly saw Mrs. Prescott in animated conversation with Rennell. She was laughing, he thought, unbecomingly, and he hated her. And he hated himself. Everything appeared in an exaggerated light to him that evening, as sometimes happened after he had had a cocktail or two; and he thought that some of the guests looked extraordinarily like the gargoyles on the *Notre Dame*. He noted with relief Ethel's entry with the sandwiches. But her flush grown redder and the gleam in her eyes grown brighter for some reason frightened him. And he didn't like the looks of Middleton at all. Not at this instant.

All parties, even the gayest, come to an end. This one also came to an end. Laughing, the guests left in ones and in couples. At last, there was no one left but Ethel. She told her mother she'd sleep that night in the gallery bedroom.

She blew out all the candles but three on the mantelpiece, and seated herself in a large chair, sinking into its cushions. The studio was silent. She sat all expectant, as if awaiting some one, her ear straining to catch every footfall on the stairs. Once she rose and paced up and down. Once she laughed hysterically. Each time she returned to the chair and, sinking into the cushions, sat expectant, impatient. . . .

At last footfalls on the stairs became audible. Impetuously, they approached nearer and nearer. There was a soft knock on the door. . . .

X

Jack called on the next afternoon at four o'clock. He had intended coming earlier, but he had gotten up with a bad headache and had fought with it all day. A headache was a rare occurrence with him. He cursed his lot, for it had been his intention to get there early and press the question of marriage. He stopped at the florist's and purchased a sizable bouquet of yellow roses; Ethel was very fond of them.

There was no answer to his knock. He sought the key under the door rug, it having been prearranged between them that on all occasions he should wait for her in the studio in the event of an appointment and she not being there punctually. He entered and, laying the flowers on the table, sat down to await her coming. He was in a fretting mood and wondered why she was not in. Then,

raising his head, his eyes rested on a letter standing up
prominently against one of the candlesticks on the mantelpiece. He rose and saw that it was addressed in her
handwriting to him. For a long time he held it in his
hands without opening it. He opened it with misgiving.
It proved to be a long letter. His eyes widened as he read
the first lines and grasped their import. Such was the
letter:

"Dearest, dearest Jack,

"My heart breaks that I should have to write these
lines to you, the dearest, kindest, noblest man in the
world. After all you've done for me, I feel like the vile
creature I am to have to hurt you of all men on this miserable planet. I am wretched, wretched, wretched. . . .
I cannot marry you.

"Yesterday I was ready to fall at your feet and wor-
ship you. Oh, if you had only encouraged me, had only
met me half way. . . . Had you but only opened your
arms out to me, without reserve, I should have been
yours. You couldn't help it, but you hesitated. In that
moment of hesitation, I discerned my unworthiness. I
saw at once, as it were in a flash, that I should never
make you happy.

"Please don't think I blame you. The fault is altogether mine. I am unstable, I have no character. Or
rather, my character in the past years has, in a new

environment, undergone changes, which have rendered me unstable. Had we, perhaps, married each other when we first loved one another—how thoroughly happy I was in those days—and grown up together, we should, I think, probably have seen the thing through, and we might still be one another's, with a couple of darling babies maybe to give sanction to continued happiness. But it's too late now! And how really wretched I am to have to hurt you!

"For you see I am no longer what I might have been. Even while I hate Paris, I love it too. I hate it for what it's made of me, a woman unfit to be your mate. In your presence I feel positively unclean. For a while I was laboring under the delusion that you could and would make me clean as yourself. Yesterday I saw my mistake. Your withdrawal in that moment of hesitation made me shrink into myself. In your silence I felt you were weighing me, questioning me. I now know I was wicked to long for just a wee little streak of wickedness in you. That would have reconciled me to you.

"I haven't told you why I love Paris. I love Paris because I do not feel my wickedness here. I don't know if I can make you understand this. But imagine me back in Biddlebury, and my position there if they found out anything about my dreadful 'past'!

"I said it was not your fault that our lovely weeks together have come to such a sad end. I now see it was inevitable. I've already told you that I was poisoned with Europe. Now I know that it is impossible for me to get Europe out of my blood. While you hesitated yesterday I had a glimmering of the truth, but was not yet sure of it. Last evening, however, settled my doubts. It was Mr. Middleton who settled them for me beyond all question and recall. I want to be honest with you. You deserve at least that!

"Please, I beg of you, do not look for me. I am leaving Paris to-day, and with Middleton, as his mistress. Far better for us both that it happened now rather than later. Please believe me! How I wish it could have been otherwise.

"Pity me if you must, but don't judge me! And may God, if there is a God, forgive me!

"Your heart-broken Ethel."

Still clutching the letter, whose significance he grasped in essence if not in detail, Jack sank down numb into the chair, a creature without life or volition. Stonified, motionless, scarcely conscious, he remained in this attitude for some time, and dim, very dim stirrings in the chaos of his mind erected before his vision fragmentary images and disjointed fancies of a haphazard helter-skelter world from which all rhyme and reason had departed and in which he himself was but a drifting particle without starting-point or goal.

How long he sat thus he did not know. It may have been minutes, or it may have been hours. Time did not matter, clocks ceased to have a meaning for him. Time can matter only in a well-ordered universe. Dimly, very dimly, he realized himself as an inconsequential fragment, in an explosion shot away into space and forever detached from other fragments which had once cohered and made him part of a none too well-ordered whole, but still a whole. Love had made the world whole for him, held its fragments in a precarious integrity. And now love had disappeared from life, and the world fell apart in a million fragments, of which he was one, falling headlong through space towards a goal invisible and unknown.

Slowly, in the reaction, warmth returned to him, suffused his centers of consciousness, and at last, with maddening force, poured out in turbulent deltas, bringing rage and self-pity and confusion to the mind, and creating an aching chaos in the heart. With a wild stare he glanced around him. The large room, with its spacious walls and high ceiling, gave him a sense of loneliness, of desolation. The very flowers, which were there in such profusion, mocked him, filled him with consternation. They had been hers, her sensitive fingers had arranged them in decorative patterns in the vases and left behind some of her grace. There was the chair in which she had sat and waited for him to speak the propitious word. And he had hesitated. How well he remembered the instants he had let pass in hesitation. And then he had opened his mouth only to speak sweet goodish words, gibberish, while she waited to hear the one firm word which would have precipitated her into his arms. Ethel was not a girl to be won with a bit of sugar. Yet, up to a point, he had won her with kindness. Kindness was not enough to hold a human being. He had lacked sense, his perfect behavior had one serious flaw: it ignored human nature, fond of its imperfections and clinging to them. Hadn't he acted throughout to gratify himself, never once thinking that woman wanted your real—oh yes, imperfect self, and not the make-believe perfect man whose part you were playing? It takes a woman to detect a man's weakness in a crisis. His peculiar strength was his weakness. He had won Ethel by kindness, and he had lost her by kindness.

"What is it all about?"

The phrase spoken aloud suddenly broke from him, involuntarily, out of the hidden recesses of himself.

"What is it all about?" he repeated.

In those weeks of growing intimacy with Ethel he believed he was getting somewhere nearer an answer. But now it was as if the doors he had seen opening, admitting him to the object of his quest, were suddenly shut in his face and barred and locked against him, once and forever.

"What is it all about?" he demanded in a still louder voice, as if he were addressing some definite personage responsible for it all.

And, as if in response to his demand, there sprang from his inner consciousness, where it seemed to lurk for his confusion, the reply his partner in business had once given him:

"Fools can ask more questions than a wise man can answer!"

"Yes, yes, yes. . . . He was a f-f-ool . . . a f-fool. . . . Once you stopped to ask questions, life uprose like a ponderous wall and confronted you with its vast impenetrable expanse. . . . Yes, yes . . . he was a fool, Jack pondered. . . . There was that wall. . . . He had heard of Indian sages who spent a lifetime contemplating a crack in a wall. . . . He was a fool. . . . His partner was a wise man. He didn't ask any questions. He earned a lot of money and put it away. He couldn't take it with him when he died. But it was pleasant to know you had it while you lived. A wise man. . . . And he, Jack Whitney, was a fool, a f-fool. . . .

There was Ethel. What was she? A fool to refuse so steady and reliable a husband, so handsome an assurance of ease and comfort for life? He pondered the riddle, and anxiously sought a solution. Over there, at home, they would have deemed her mad. Only the other day he had read in a newspaper of a poor girl who in Kansas or some other Western state was sent by a judge to an insane asylum, because, though without a penny, she bluntly refused to marry a man with a million!

It wasn't as if she loathed him. Yesterday she was ready to marry him. Why, why had she acted as she did? At home they would have called her a wastrel! "Poisoned with Europe," she had said. What did she mean? His mind desperately sought a co-relation between these facts. She had also talked much of life, of her intense desire to live life. What was life? What connection had it with being a wastrel, and with Europe? There was, undoubtedly, some intimate connection. What was it? His questing fingers groped in the darkness of his mind. ... Light after light flared for him, and became extinguished before he could get a glimpse of the truth. ...

The image of Europe persisted: Europe, a wastrel, her veins rich with blood and wine, pouring herself out in an irresponsible happy-go-luck, devil-may-care, no-thought-of-to-morrow debauch! ...

"What is it all about?" the question once more formed itself on his lips, persisting with the stubborn determination of incurable folly.

And again and again the personal loss obtruded itself on his consciousness, dimming it with heart-ache, preventing clear vision.

Thus, hour after hour, unconscious of time, he sat

waging a struggle, contending as it were with the devil, and no issue in sight. . . .

Then, suddenly, out of the brooding darkness of himself, as it were in a flash of lightning, he saw the bottomless depth of the abyss on whose brink he stood. Below there, unmindful of good and evil, of wise men and fools, life ran on in a turbulent stream. . . . On its banks stood men and women gesticulating and, with rapture, flung themselves in, sacrificial victims to a pagan god. . . .

It was really an old tale, and as a child he had read it in his school-book of Greek legends: its hero was Zeus, in the shape of a bull; its heroine Europa . . . that seductive goddess, loved by gods and men to their distraction and ruin. All life was a preparation for death. Europa was dying and her own and her adopted children were dutifully and affectionately performing their *danse macabre*.

THE SAMOVAR

I

Ivan Petroff's custom, since becoming a widower, was to leave the lumber-yard, of which he was the owner, precisely at four o'clock each day and to wend his way home, where a hot samovar awaited him with a punctuality not less exact. A samovar, as every good Russian knows, is, if a comfort, not the same thing as a wife, even though it take turns at being hot and cold, at humming a song and keeping silent, at shining brightly on gala days—reflecting gladness—and being dully irresponsive on others. Nevertheless, since his wife's death, Petroff—or Ivan Stepanitch, as he was familiarly called —resisted the importunities of matchmakers: one might as well have asked him to have another samovar in the place of the one he had. Petroff had chosen the samovar with great care, just as he had chosen his lamented wife with great care. The one he saw in a shop window—the samovar, of course—the other behind a shop counter: nothing strange, to be sure, in either fact. How often he had passed that window and paused to look at the samovar. There was something about it that struck his fancy, just as later there was something about the woman he had married that struck his fancy. It was not shaped quite like other samovars; or rather, this particular samovar had a shape, others hadn't. Other samovars had a straight up and down effect, without any curves or deviations in the body to make the thing interesting and piquant to the eye; this samovar curved in at the middle like a Greek urn or a finely-shaped woman's waist. Though Petroff was far from being a *barin* (a noble), he somehow had an eye for these things: a fact which imparted a measure of confirmation to the report of his grandmother having been the illegitimate daughter of a *barin* in the neighborhood. One day, after a long wooing of that samovar, unable any longer to resist the ever urging possessive instinct, he walked into the shop and at his request the young woman behind the counter went to the window and, lifting the desired object high with both her hands—a maneuver which set off the young woman's shapeliness—put it tenderly on the counter. The whole effect was of a woman lifting a baby under the arms; at least so it seemed to Ivan Petroff. She smilingly looked down on the samovar and waited for Petroff to speak.

"How much?" muttered Petroff.

The young woman named the price.

"Rather high, isn't it?" said Petroff.

"I've got some at half the price," replied the young woman, still smiling. "But, of course, they are not the same thing. Look at the shape—the sparkle too! One in a thousand—"

"Y-yes— I see—" murmured Petroff, not looking at all at the samovar. He was actually, in a half-dazed way, realizing the background. He somehow, as yet vaguely, grasped that she, in her tight-fitting black frock, set off the samovar; the thought that they were like two pieces of a set stunned him. Yes, one in a thousand!

"I'll t-take it," he said at last hesitatingly, and slowly pulled out his wallet.

"Name and address, please!"

"Oh!—Ivan—"

"Ivan—" repeated the young woman after him, writing at the same time.

"Deuce take it! How prettily she says it!" thought Petroff, while she, pencil in hand, patiently waited.

"Ivan—" she repeated, noting his absent look and wishing to give him his cue.

"That's right," he said, "Ivan—Ivan Ste-pa-nitch— I mean Stepanovitch—"

"Ivan Stepanovitch—" she repeated after him, and waited again.

"Pet-roff—"

"Ivan Stepanovitch Petroff—" she pronounced, gathering up all the fragments of his name, and added: "And what is your address?"

"Never mind!" he exclaimed suddenly. "I'll come back for it myself. But please give me a receipt."

Once in the street, Petroff drew out the receipt and read under the firm's name: "per Anna Svetloff." That was what he wanted the receipt for; he was afraid she would sign only her initials.

That was the worst about taking a fancy to a thing: in the end you wanted it. He now had his samovar. But how could he tell when he unwarily entered the shop that day that his small innocent fancy would breed a greater, an infinitely more difficult one of satisfaction, since merely to admire there was need of something more than the stopping before the shop-window; one had to go into the shop itself; moreover, one must go in to buy something. So Petroff began to frequent that shop on one pretext or another. The second time he went to the shop he bought a mouse-trap, though he already had three lying idle on the rummage-heap in the attic. On his third visit he bought a fishing-rod: goodness alone knew what he was going to fish for: all the fishing he'd ever done had been in dreams. His next venture was a tin-opener. He went on buying these things, and as a result of his otherwise useless purchases had achieved the privilege of calling her familiarly, "Anna Pavlovna."

One day a strong impulse urged Petroff towards Anna Pavlovna. It was the same impulse, only ten thousand times stronger, that finally drove him to possess the samovar. Had it been one of those devilishly clever Frenchmen we hear of who had been thus in love, he would have asked the object of his affections out for a walk and deftly maneuvered her towards a fashionable dressmaking establishment, where pausing and allowing her eyes to fall on the nice feminine things in the shop-window, until her mouth had begun to water, he would have remarked with discreet casualness: "What do you say, dear, to going in and ordering a trousseau?" Then there is the case of the Spaniard, who put the question with equal effectiveness: "Shall you and I put our clothes in the same trunk and go on a long journey together?" Unfortunately our Ivan Petroff was not up to these clever French and Spanish tricks. He was a simple Russian, with honest, if sometimes uncouth ways; nevertheless, with an eye, as it has already been observed, for the little niceties of life. He had not forgotten how nice she had looked behind the samovar, how one had set the other off, how much they seemed like two companion pieces of a set. Such was the picture she evoked, a picture which with the passing of days had grown tense and luminous, almost too large for the frame of his mind, which it threatened to split. So, having decided to speak to her, he approached her thus:

"Anna Pavlovna, you remember the samovar I bought of you?"

"Why shouldn't I remember it? It was such a nice one. I was quite sorry to part with it."

"That's just what I came to talk to you about. You needn't be parted from it. I came to ask you if you wouldn't come and pour tea for me?—I mean for always—"

There was a silence. Petroff was afraid that she would say that she had already promised to pour tea for some one else. She looked serious for a while, then burst out laughing.

"What an original way you have of putting it, Ivan Stepanitch! Who could resist it? Of course, I'll come and pour tea for you. But tell me, Ivan Stepanitch, what did you buy a mouse-trap for—and a fishing-rod—and a bird-cage—and a monkey-wrench—and a tin-opener—and a— You didn't really want any of those things, did you?"

Petroff smiled assent shyly.

"Remember the day you bought the bird-cage?" asked Anna Pavlovna, and he nodding in the affirmative she went on: "You were going to say something to me that day, weren't you?" He again nodding in the affirmative she continued: "Yes, I watched you, Ivan Stepanitch. I watched you, as you looked through the wires of the cage. You were looking at me. You said nothing. But your eyes gave you away— You've got fine eyes, Ivan Stepanitch— Come nearer, Ivan Stepanitch—" And Ivan Stepanovitch drawing nearer, she impulsively seized his head between her hands, and kissed his eyes. "Don't you try," she said, laughing, "to fool a woman so long as you have those eyes. Of course, I'll come and pour tea for you!"

And so Ivan Stepanovitch took her home to pour tea for him. For a full year Anna Pavlovna poured tea for her Ivan. Then, one day she fell ill, and for days lay in a delirium, with intervals of calm. During one of these, the nurse, all in white, poured out a cup of tea for her patient: for the samovar, on the insistent demands of the patient, was now in the sick-room. Anna Pavlovna watched the nurse pouring out tea, and imagined that the white figure was Death.

"No, no!" she cried, as the white figure approached her with a cup of tea. "Take it away! Don't make me drink it! I don't want to die! No, no—not just yet!"

II

Ivan Petroff's custom since becoming a widower—so our story began, you will remember—was to leave the lumber-yard, of which he was the owner, precisely at four o'clock each day, when he would wend his way home, where a hot samovar awaited him. Neighbors, on seeing him pass by, regulated their clocks by him (as the saying goes), so punctual were his goings and comings. Punctuality is not natural to a Russian, but Petroff was punctual. It is not to be wondered at, then, that he was regarded as a queer sort. Not that Petroff was business-like. Far from it. His punctuality was rather the result of apathy, become mechanical. He had been like that since his wife died. That had happened a year ago.

A samovar has much to answer for in Russian life. If

it were not for samovars there might not be any Russian
novels. This particular samovar had much to answer for
in Petroff's life. The first day that he was unfaithful to
it was the day that began Petroff's second adventure.

On leaving the lumber-yard that day, Ivan Petroff
walked as usual as far as the church, where the road
forked into two. As usual, he took off his hat and crossed
himself. Then he did something unusual. Instead of
taking the road to the right, as was his habit of over a
year, he turned into the road to the left. An instant before he had no idea of turning to the left. He had no idea
why he had turned into the road to the left. It was as if
a magnet which had formerly drawn him to the right had
now changed its position in the road to the left. Petroff
himself had hardly realized what he had done until he
felt a slap on his back and heard a familiar voice say:

"And what brings you this way, Ivan Stepanitch?"

Ivan Petroff looked at his questioner in a confused
way and stammered:

"—I?—I? I'm just taking a walk—"

Petroff blushed. He could not lie gracefully. All the
same, if he had wished to tell the truth, he could not have
said just what took him that way and not the other way.
But he felt a strong consciousness of unfaithfulness, a
desire to get away from his own beloved samovar, which
never ceased to remind him of the dear one, who, daily,
for a whole year, had poured his tea out of it.

At the next turn of the road was the inn, and thither he guiltily directed his footsteps, as in the old days, before he had married Anna Pavlovna.

He paid but slight attention to the sleigh at the door, nor to the woman getting out of it, all wrapped in furs.

"Well, well, you haven't honored us with your company for a long while," said the proprietor, greeting his former patron heartily.

"A *samovarchik* (a little samovar), please!" said Petroff with an embarrassed air, "and how are you, Pavel Timofeyevitch?"

A little samovar was brought, containing a mere fifteen tumblers, a small matter for a Russian, and our Ivan Petroff, removing his fur overcoat and his high fur cap, and undoing his caftan, sat down before the tea urn. Before pouring out the tea he gulped down a small vodka as a kind of appetizer.

In the Russian manner he put a small lump of sugar in his mouth and sipped the tea through it. He was drinking his third tumbler, when a woman, the same he had casually noted getting out of the sleigh, entered the inn. She surveyed the room, for an instant fixed Petroff with her eyes, and sat down at a table across the room, facing him. Apparently, she was staying there, for she did not have her furs with her. She also ordered a small samovar.

All of a sudden Petroff felt strongly conscious of the woman's presence, and on raising his eyes found hers fixed on his. And helplessly he felt his soul wrenched from his body with a kind of violence, drawn by the unfathomable power of those eyes. Then, she relinquished his soul and allowed it to drift back, now hers.

There was something about that woman which reminded him, indefinably at first, of his lamented wife. There was, indeed, some similarity in their features, but the stranger's eyes were larger, more widely parted, and had a sense of knowledge and worldliness which the other's did not possess, and this was an added attraction. At all events, the superficial resemblance was in itself sufficiently startling to cause a flutter, and more than a flutter, in Ivan's heart, as his eyes, involuntarily, continued to drift in her direction, always to find her eyes responding with an intimate wonderment, as if to say: "I surely have seen you somewhere before? But whether I have seen you or not does not matter. I know you!"

In short, they were all-knowing eyes, and he felt them sounding him to the innermost depths of his being. Intent as that look was, it was not a stare, for there was no hardness in it; indeed, it had all the tremulous modulation of pliant violin music stealing into one's heart without one knowing how. An inner fluid warmth, such as he had not remembered since his first courting of Anna, and surely not to be ascribed to tea, was stealing through Petroff and flooding him. It began to radiate from his moistened eyes and to wander in vapory, lit-up clouds, which seemed to interpose themselves between him and the woman, so that he saw her as through a filmy mist. Such havoc can a woman play with a man's soul!

Stranger still, Petroff felt that the woman was undergoing a not unsimilar emotion. More than once, prodded by an inexplicable impulse, he was on the point of rising and asking her to join him at his samovar, but Petroff was a very shy man, and he could not screw up his courage to commit a possible effrontery to the unknown woman for whom, at first sight, he had contracted so tender a regard.

After two hours, poor Petroff paid the waiter and reluctantly took his departure. He felt the woman's eyes follow him until he had passed through the door, and immediately formed a mental resolution:

"I shall be here to-morrow at the same time. Deuce take it, I wish I had spoken to her!"

It would be as hard to say why Petroff made this sudden resolution as it would be to say what drew him here in the first place. Such was Petroff, such things happened to Petroff. Why inquire further?

At all events, on arriving home, he astonished the already wondering maid, Marusya, by instructing her not to prepare the samovar the next day, so that poor Marusya crossed herself and muttered:

"What's come over master? I hope nothing ill. The Saints preserve him!"

Petroff lay wide awake that night, and a woman's eyes, gray as a sunless sea, long eyelashes flickering, looked at him and beckoned out of the darkness, it was hard to tell whether to paradise or perdition.

Willingly, it is true, yet helplessly, Petroff at the same hour the next day wended his way towards the inn. He felt sure she would be there, yet feared that she might not. There was no one in the room. He took the seat he had occupied the previous day, ordered a samovar, and waited, waited— At last he heard the sound of a woman's voice, and knew at once it was hers. Palpitating instants became transformed in his heart into hammer-beats. That voice, indeed, though he had not heard it before, matched those eyes well. She was ordering a samovar. She glided into the room with a feline motion, and the brown fur of her long overcoat undulated to the rhythm of her body, and might have been integrally a part of her. She sat down in her former seat, and Petroff sat still and rigid in his, a serpent charmed. It was the same as yesterday, and Petroff could not screw up his courage to rise and speak. This time, having consulted her watch, she was the first to rise from the table and, departing, left Petroff a prey to the most agitated emotions.

For three days this little comedy was enacted, and on the fourth Petroff made up his mind to speak, come what will. After the sixth tumbler of tea, Petroff began to curse himself. The charming unknown did not come.

"I've missed my chance, the deuce take it!" he muttered to himself. "That's what comes of being a ninny and putting things off!"

At six o'clock he rose, and with a crestfallen air walked out of the room, feeling like a whipped hungry dog, his tail between his legs.

"Perhaps to-morrow!" he murmured half-hopefully.

Listlessly he arrived at his own door. Having deposited his hat and coat in the ante-room, he entered the dining room. He found it lit up and the table set for dinner. He flung himself down on the sofa and gazed towards the table. A singular fact, which had at first escaped his notice, now, quite suddenly, impressed itself upon his consciousness, as he scratched his head in astonishment. The table was set for two! He sat up and looked again. There was no mistake. The table was set for two! He had not remembered having asked any one to dinner. Indeed, he had not asked any one to dinner since his wife had died.

What was the meaning of this? Petroff sat up and rubbed his eyes. A mood of enchantment held him and prevented him from calling Marusya. There was a temptation to discover the meaning of the illusion, if illusion it was, for himself. A thought slowly struggled in his simple brain, a sluggish, yet a wild thought— But that was impossible—simply impossible— He was a fool and a simpleton to entertain such a thought. His blood began to tingle through his veins hotly; afterwards, from head to foot, he trembled with the ague. He wondered: was he ill, was fever setting in, or had the woman cast an evil spell upon him? And he remembered that he hadn't slept three nights. He had better have Marusya call a doctor. What was the good of a doctor? There was no remedy against a woman's eyes. There they were, even at that instant, between the half-parted draperies in the doorway, looking at him, penetrating him to the bottom of his soul.

She was real as life, and it was the first time that he had seen her hatless, showing a wealth of brown hair, rich with gold-tinged highlights. It was wound round her head in large, tight, snaky coils, and under her broad high-arched brows her grave, long-lashed eyes were lapsing into a smile. She appeared to hold the draperies together with an invisible hand, and only her head showed through the opening.

Petroff sat transfixed, unable to move or say a word. He feared that if he stirred the vision would vanish.

The smile between the draperies broadened. Then the invisible hand flung aside the draperies, and the figure ran forward and dropped on its knees before Petroff.

"Here am I, Ivan Stepanitch. You have wanted me, and I have come!"

Petroff said nothing. He was dazed and under a spell.

"You did want me, did you not?" she went on, as her hand sought his knees and rested quietly there.

"Yes—" replied Petroff, galvanized by that touch into life. "But how do you know my name? Who are you, and where do you come from?"

"Don't ask questions, Ivan Stepanitch. But if you'd like to know, a little bird told me. As for my name, call me Maria Feodorovna. Aren't you glad I have come?"

Petroff shyly put his hands on her shoulders.

"I'm real enough," laughed Maria Feodorovna.

"I am not dreaming?—"

"You may kiss me when you wake up— Then we'll have some dinner. I am frightfully hungry. I've asked Marusya to cook something especially nice."

"I have not slept three nights because of you," said Petroff, stroking her hair.

"And you are not going to sleep a fourth," laughed Maria Feodorovna. "Poor Ivan!"

"You don't mean that you are going to leave me," exclaimed Petroff, alarm in his voice.

"No, of course not, you stupid! What I meant was that I have come to stay. You do want me?"

In answer, he seized one of her hands and covered it with kisses.

III

Who was she? Where had she come from? What had been her past? Ivan never knew. Every time he questioned her, during their lovings, she simply laughed and replied:

"What does it matter, darling? You are happy, aren't you? People who are happy shouldn't ask questions. Just imagine I've dropped down from heaven, and take your happiness. Did I ask questions when I first saw you? I didn't even ask you whether I might come or not. I liked you at first sight, and I knew that you liked me. That was enough. And so I just came—"

But the male in him, jealous of her past history, was not satisfied, and he importuned her:

"But did you—I mean are you a widow? Are you—"

She always stopped a question with a kiss and the remonstrance:

"Don't ask questions. Questions bring unhappiness— They are always the beginning of all trouble."

Three months they lived as man and wife, and were happy together. She turned a deaf ear to his repeated proposals of marriage. She placed all such proposals in the category of unnecessary questions.

"There you go again with your questions! Aren't we happy as we are? What do you want to marry me for. Besides—"

She always paused there, just as he felt he was on the eve of a revelation, which might furnish the key to the mystery of her. But having said, "Besides—," she would scrutinize the eager, questioning face of her lover, and, after a pause, break into a tantalizing laugh.

"Never mind, Ivan. It doesn't matter so long as we are happy— It doesn't really matter."

Under her caresses, Petroff would forget everything, to return afterwards to an intense preoccupation with that portentous "Besides." He felt sure that there was much behind that enigmatic word, and his mind was troubled. Had she run away from a husband? Was she not free to marry him? He was fiercely in love with Maria Feodorovna, and he thought that if she would only consent to marry him, he would secure her for ever. But there was always that "Besides!"

One evening a strange thing happened. It was winter.

THE AUTHOR OF "WANDERING WOMEN"

John Cournos is an American writer, born in Russia, whose literary career was shaped and developed as a resident of London.

He was born in 1881 in a Ukrainian village. The medical tradition was strong in his family and it was decided that he, too, was to become a doctor. But his parents lost their money and with their large family emigrated to Philadelphia when John was ten. He attended public school for four years, selling newspapers in his spare hours. At the age of fourteen his schooling was terminated when he went to work as a mill hand. Two years in the mills and he became an office boy on a Philadelphia paper.

For the next fifteen years he was a Philadelphia newspaperman. Here his first interest in literature developed in his acquaintance with art students and his first literary efforts consisted of art criticism. At thirty-one as the assistant editor of a Sunday supplement he abruptly gave up his position and left for London.

"I was in a rut," he wrote about his self-imposed exile years later, "and felt if something didn't happen I should end by cutting my throat. Instead I chucked a perfectly good life-time job and came to England without any introductions or prospects. I haven't any idea how I managed to hold on nor need I go into details as to the life of a friendless free-lance in London. All the while I was accomplishing the main object of my stay, for I learnt English on English soil."

These early London days crystallized his urge to write a novel about which he had been thinking for years, and at thirty-five he began "The Mask" (1919). Instead of one book the theme broadened and the story was continued in "The Wall" (1921) and "Babel" (1922). His fourth novel, "The New Candide" (1924) was his first venture in the purely imaginative field, marking his release from the experiences, chronicled in his trilogy which drove him to write in the first place.

Besides a tremendous amount of critical writing which has appeared in leading English and American journals (Mr. Cournos is considered one of the leading literary critics in England) his other published work includes: novels—"Miranda Masters" (1926), "O'Fla-

herty the Great" (1927); poems—"In Exile" (1923);
biography—"A Modern Plutarch" (1928); plays—
"Sport of Gods" (1925). He has also done extensive
translations from the Russian.

He was a member of the Commission sent to Russia
by the British Foreign Office in 1917-18 and later was
on the staff of the Ministry of Information. In 1920 he
was a member of the commission investigating food
conditions in the famine areas of Central Europe.

A few years ago Mr. Cournos returned to this country, taking up his residence in New Haven, Connecticut, where the present book was written.

A new PAPER BOOK is published and mailed to subscribers on the 25th of each month. The first book in the series was published in September 1929. In May, THE BRIDGE OF SAN LUIS REY by Thornton Wilder was set up and printed as an example of the format.

Cover design for this book by John Barbour.

NOTICE OF CHANGE OF ADDRESS *should include the old address as well as the new, and be printed plainly to obviate error. We must have notice at least six weeks before it can be effected.*

Subscription prices for PAPER BOOKS: *one year, for Continental United States of America* $5.00; *elsewhere* $6.00 SINGLE COPIES, 50 *cents each mailed postpaid to any address.*

Charles Boni PAPER BOOKS *New York*
Number 80 *Fifth Avenue*

☆   ☆   ☆

The following reprints have been issued in format similar to
PAPER BOOKS. Copies will be sent postpaid to any address on receipt of 50 cents each.

The History of Mr. Polly	H. G. Wells
Tar	Sherwood Anderson
Michelangelo	Romain Rolland
The Lost Girl	D. H. Lawrence
The Captain's Doll	D. H. Lawrence
The Personal Relation in Industry	John D. Rockefeller, Jr.
The Hard-Boiled Virgin	Frances Newman
Open All Night	Paul Morand
Cheri	Colette
Our Changing Morality	Bertrand Russell and others
What Is Wrong with Marriage	Hamilton and MacGowan
Kept	Alec Waugh
Against the Grain	J. K. Huysmans
Our Business Civilization	James Truslow Adams
The Cardinal's Mistress	Benito Mussolini
My University Days	Maxim Gorky
This Earth of Ours	Jean-Henri Fabre
The Wonder Book of Chemistry	Jean-Henri Fabre
Why Men Fight	Bertrand Russell
The Story of the Irish Nation	Francis Hackett
Israel	Ludwig Lewisohn